M. M. B.

Glenmorven, or, Child Life in the Highlands

M. M. B.

Glenmorven, or, Child Life in the Highlands

ISBN/EAN: 9783337160746

Printed in Europe, USA, Canada, Australia, Japan

Cover: Foto ©Andreas Hilbeck / pixelio.de

More available books at **www.hansebooks.com**

GLENMORVEN

OR

CHILD LIFE IN THE HIGHLANDS.

BY M. M. B.

EDINBURGH:
THE EDINBURGH PUBLISHING COMPANY.
LONDON: SIMPKIN, MARSHALL, & CO.

1878.

Dedicated

TO

Mrs JOHN FISCHER,

WITH LOVE AND RESPECT,

BY

THE AUTHOR.

CONTENTS.

———

GLENMORVEN;

OR,

CHILD LIFE IN THE HIGHLANDS.

———◆———

CAMPING OUT.

CHAPTER I.

I HAVE a number of little nephews and nieces whom I often go to see, and nothing delights them so much as hearing stories. I had told them every story I could think of, from time-honoured Cinderella to the last new Christmas book ; I had turned novels and plays into childish tales ; but still they cried for more. I then tried the plan of telling an old story in a new form ; but they soon found me out, and it was, "Auntie, you have told us that before, we know that already." At last, quite driven to despair, I said I would tell them a story from real life.

"And one that is quite, quite true?" said Nina, with big eyes. "Yes, it is quite, quite true."

"Now Bertie, keep very still on the sofa ; and Janet, you can sit on this footstool. . Don't interrupt me or speak to me, for fear I shall stop ; and once I stop, you may perhaps never be able to make me go on again, any more than the nursery clock you were all trying your hand at."

"But nurse made it go on," said Bertie.

"Yes, after getting a man to put it right," said Nina grandly, for she had had nothing to do with putting it wrong, "and it took him two days."

"But it will not take me two days, but two weeks, to be set on again, so I would advise you not to stop me, but all to sit quite still."

Long, long ago, before in fact any of you were born, there lived two little girls called Bel and Fan. They were twins : that is, they were born on the same day, and therefore were exactly the same age. When they were babies, they were so much alike, that it was almost impossible to tell which was which. Even their mother sometimes mistook them, and their nurse was obliged to tie up Bel's sleeves with blue ribbon and Fan's with red, to prevent mistakes.

As they grew bigger, they began to show a little difference. Both had thick fair hair, large gray eyes, and the same complexion ; but Bell was much taller and stouter, and had not such a fine nose as Fan. Fan, in fact, was much the prettier of the two, only rather thin and wiry ; but neither of them cared very much about being pretty. It is only vain little girls that do that ; and though the twins were not so good as they might have been, they were not vain. No, they never thought at all of how they looked, although they were ten years of age—older than you, Nina.

They lived in a wild place, far away among great hills, with their uncle and aunts; and at the time I speak of, had been there some years. Such a lovely wild place, full of large rocks and high trees, inviting one to climb. Indeed, that was one thing Bel and Fan could do very well, particularly Fan, who, being light and active, could clamber up a rock like a goat, or scramble up a tree like a squirrel.

The twins were born in India, and had been sent home when they were five years old. They had a brother called Tom, a little younger than themselves, and a still younger brother and sister had since joined them at their uncle's.

You wish to know the name of the place, Nina? Well, it was Glenmorven.

The house was large and old-fashioned, and stood on a terrace at one side of a lovely green valley or glen winding between high and steep mountains. About a mile off was the sea, and a beautiful wide bay. The beach was mostly sand and pebbles, but here and there were large rocks. Across the bay one saw more mountains—some near, some far, far away. Close to the shore was Glenmorven village; from it a high road ran up one side of the glen, passing close to Glenmorven House.

"What was their uncle's name?" you ask, Bertie. Their uncle was Mr Farquhar. He lived upon the family estate in the West Highlands; his wife was dead, and three sisters lived with him: Aunt Margaret, rather elderly; Aunt Isa, nearly as old; and Aunt Kate, still young.

Mr Farquhar took the kindest interest in all his dependants, built them good houses, and kept up good schools. He was always ready to give advice and assistance to his poor neighbours, and large numbers of persons came daily to consult him—some from a great distance. Though not rich, he was quite a public benefactor, and was known and esteemed over the whole country.

As I have said, Glenmorven House was large and old-fashioned. At one side of it was a square garden within stone walls, containing numbers of gooseberry, raspberry, and currant bushes, strawberry beds, and borders of flowers. A door from its lower end led into a tree-garden or orchard. Here were apple, pear, and cherry trees. Think how delightful a place this was for children in a good fruit season! Sometimes, indeed, the naughty blackbirds and thrushes ate up all the cherries, and the spring frosts nipped the pears and apples. But the gooseberries, rasps, and currants never failed, even in the wettest season, when one had to go and gather them under an umbrella!

On the other side of the house, the ground sloped gently down to a river which flowed through pretty meadows. From the house to the high road ran a short avenue, and a little way off were the stables, farmyard, and some cottars' houses.

Ah! that was a charming country for children to live in. There was always so much to do, and so much to amuse one. The only dull days were the very, very wet ones, or when one had a cold; and even then, one could draw, or paint pictures, or cut things out in paper. I cannot say that Bel and Fan read much, and they had very few toys, and did not care much for dolls.

On Christmas and birthdays, their aunts gave them needle-books, or pin-cushions, or some such home-made little things, as there were no toy-shops at Glenmorven.

Once a-year, indeed, their mother sent them a box from India, with beautiful things, richly embroidered white dresses, red or green scarfs, with silk flowers of all colours; gold filigree ornaments as fine as lace, or silver bangles or armlets. But these things were far too fine to play with, or indeed to wear, and after being looked at and admired, were always carefully packed away, so the twins did not care much for them.

Twice a-year, a fair or market was held in Glenmorven, and on these days their uncle always gave them a little money. With this they used to go as near the market-place as they dared, for there were always numbers of

cows and horses there, and at some old woman's stall
purchase a few sweeties or sugar-plums of bright colours
but doubtful wholesomeness. There was nothing else to
buy, but it made them feel quite important to have
money to spend. Out of doors, they had a hundred
ways of amusing themselves. They usually had pets
that had to be fed or looked at ; they had little gardens,
which they were expected to keep in order, but I am
afraid they were not so tidy as they might have been.
Then there were the stables and the farmyard, where
there were horses and cows to pet, a Turkey cock to
tease and be a little afraid of, calves to chase, and pigs
to look at.

Behind the farmyard rose a high hill, delightful to
climb, down whose sides rushed and tumbled a wild
burn.

The river, too, afforded endless amusement. In summer one could wade about barefoot in the warm water ;
or build stone piers, or make islands ; or catch eels or
tiny trout. Or one could play for hours with the smooth
prettily marked pebbles, choosing some to be cows and
others to be sheep, and enclosing them in parks and
fields, made by laying rows of stones along the clean
white sand.

Then there was the sea ! That was a rarer, if a greater
pleasure. On calm, hot summer days, they, their little
brothers and sister, nurse, and sometimes the aunts,

went in a pony cart to the seaside.   There they were allowed to bathe ; after which how good the contents of the luncheon basket tasted !   There were many wonderful things at the sea-shore—sea-urchins, starfish, and animals like flowers.   It was quite Fairyland !

CHAPTER II.

"Had the twins no papa?" you ask, Bertie. Yes, they had a papa. Mr Farquhar had two brothers. The eldest, who was called Kenneth, had been many years an officer in India, and was married to an English wife. These were the papa and mamma of the twins. The other brother was called Charles, and was a lawyer in Edinburgh.

"And had they no lessons to learn?" you ask, Nina. Well, they once had lessons, and I am now coming to something very naughty about the twins.

When they first came to Glenmorven, their aunts had taught them; afterwards they had a governess, called Miss Murray. Her father had been killed in battle in India, and the small pension his two children had was just enough to enable the son to finish his education for the Church. So the daughter resolved to support herself as a governess, until her brother should get a parish living.

The aunts, who had been at school with her, had begged her to come and teach the twins. She was very handsome and accomplished, patient and good-tempered, so every one was very fond of her. The twins were generally very docile and good in the schoolroom, especially in winter or wet weather; but in the long summer days they were always rather inattentive.

Some months before the time I am going to tell you of, young Mr Murray had got a very good living at Dunard, about ten miles from Glenmorven. He was impatient for his sister to come to him, and put his house in order, and make her home with him. But Miss Murray being fond of the children, and much interested in them, did not intend to leave until some suitable person had been found to fill her place.

This particular summer was a very hot one. The twins began to get quite careless and even rebellious. They used to gaze out of the schoolroom windows, and long to be out on the hill-side, and quite neglected their lessons. Tommy and the little sister were in the schoolroom too, and they also began to be troublesome, and grumble at having lessons to do ! My dears, there is nothing so easily copied as a bad example ! When the twins became naughty, the younger ones became naughty too.

No doubt it was rather tiresome to be declining French verbs, practising Weber's last waltz, or doing sums in vulgar fractions, when the sun was so bright, and there were so many delightful things to be done out of doors. But children are young only once in their lives, and if they do not learn then, they will become ignorant men and women.

At one o'clock the children dined, when the grown-up people had their lunch, and then played about for an hour. At half-past two o'clock the large dinner-bell used to be rung to call them back to lessons. It had happened several times lately that the bell had been rung for them in vain. Some hours later they would arrive, laden with ferns and wildflowers, and saying, " They had just gone a short way up the burn, or just a little way up the glen ; they did not know how late it was ; " quite penitent, and promising to be more mindful again. But it was quite a chance but that next day they did the same ; and so Miss Murray began to find it difficult to forgive them.

At last, Miss Murray's patience was quite exhausted. She would have liked to have made them learn the last page of Weber's last waltz, and to have seen them a little more perfect in the French verbs ; but she felt, while they were so idle, she was only wasting her time ; so one day she packed up her boxes and made ready to leave. The children shed many tears and gave her many damp kisses at parting, for they loved her very much. She comforted them a little by promising to come soon and see them, and by saying, that when her brother's manse should be in order, she would have them to pay her a visit at Dunard.

Well ! Miss Murray was gone ; and as you can easily understand, the twins had no more lessons.

Their aunts had each her own interests and occupations. Aunt Margaret had charge of the housekeeping. Aunt Isa was delicate, and spent a great deal of her time in making fine lace, or in reading poetry ; for she was rather romantic. Aunt Kate was clever, lively, and fond of society, and her time was taken up in entertaining the visitors, of whom the house was always full in summer and autumn.

An old Scotch nurse, who had been with them since the twins came home from India, ruled the children in the nursery ; but Bel and Fan had long left her kingdom, and now they were absolutely free. Yes ! they were free !

At first they could not quite believe it ; but when they did, they took full advantage of it.

All through the long days of the summer months they ran quite wild. The only check upon them was, that when they were not in time for dinner, they had to go without ; and that when they tore their clothes, they had to expect a scold from nurse.

But, poor twins ! they little thought, that when they were wearing out Miss Murray's patience, and gaining their long holiday, they had been preparing a worse imprisonment for themselves ; as you shall presently hear. Naughtiness never goes unpunished.

One morning, after the arrival of the post-bag, their aunts called them into the breakfast-room, and told them with much importance that their father and mother had landed in England, and would soon arrive on a visit to Glenmorven. I cannot say that the twins were very happy at the news; in fact, I believe they forgot it after a few minutes, for they scarcely remembered their parents. They could just recall a tall, dark gentleman, in an officer's uniform, called papa ; and a fair, beautifully dressed lady, called mamma, who used to lie on a sofa, and did not like them to go very close to her, for fear of crushing her flounces.

They had, no doubt, often heard their uncle and aunts speak of their parents, and they knew these beautiful presents came from them. Also, when under Miss Murray's rule, they used regularly to send them letters, written with great care, and signed " Your dutiful and affectionate daughters."

But one could not expect them to be really fond of such far-away parents, or to love them, as you children, for instance, love your dear papa and mamma, who are always with you, and always doing things to please and amuse you.

Not that Colonel and Mrs Farquhar did not often think of their little girls ; indeed, the first thing they said to each other, on seeing the shores of England, was, " Now, please God, we shall see our children ! " But

the twins did not know this—only that their parents had
arrived in England ; and then they went off together to
look for blaeberries in a certain burn they knew off,
and forgot all about it !

About a fortnight after this, the twins had been up all
morning on the hill-side finishing a dam. You want to
know what that is, Nina ? Well, the children wished to
make a pond. Had the ground been flat, they would only
have had to dig a hole near water ; but as their pond was
on sloping ground. they had to build a strong wall of earth
on the low side to keep in the water : that was the dam.
This had been their work all morning—"puddling" in
mud and water ; and very hot and dirty, you may be sure,
they were ; but very happy, for the dam was finished,
and held in water beautifully.

In the pond they meant to keep a few trout, after first
catching them in the river.

It suddenly struck them when their work was done,
that it must be dinner-time, as they felt very hungry,
so they raced down the hill like two wild-goats. When
they reached the avenue, they saw a carriage stop at the
gate, with a lady and gentleman in it.

" Here ! you little girl ! open the gate, will you ? "
cried the gentleman ; and as Bel held it open, he threw
her a sixpence, and drove on to the house.

Bel was very much astonished ; not at having been
asked to open the gate, but at having had a piece of

money thrown to her. It was the first time such a thing had happened to her. Everybody far and near knew who she was, however dirty and untidy she might appear. I must say she felt much offended.

"I wonder who these people can be, Fan? Strangers of course. Just fancy! throwing me a sixpence, as if I were a beggar! I'm sure they are English. I wonder very much who they are."

"Perhaps they are Aunt Kate's English friends whom she was visiting in Spring," said Fan. "Did you notice that was the dogcart and old mare from Dunard Inn? They must have come across the hill."

"Let us go in by the kitchen, Fan, that we may not meet them," said Bel.

So the twins went slowly round by a field behind the avenue, and got into the house, unobserved, by the back entrance.

CHAPTER III.

IN the kitchen there was a great to do. The cook and other servants bustling about preparing lunch, were far too busy to answer questions ; but just then nurse looked in, and called out in an excited manner—

"There you be at last, Miss Bel and Miss Fan ! and bonnie like tickets ye are ! Come awa up-stairs, and get yoursels dressed. There's your papa and mamma come this instant frae the Indies, and askin' after ye. A pretty like sight ye baith are. There's no a preen to choose atween ye," continued she, as she hurried them up-stairs.

The twins felt quite bewildered, and submitted patiently to being undressed, washed, brushed, and then arrayed in clean dresses. While she was dressing them, nurse told them that their parents had not been expected for some days, and then by the weekly steamer; but that, instead of waiting for the steamer, they had posted from the last railway station, and that on getting to Dunard, and finding no other carriage and no driver at hand, Colonel Farquhar had resolved to drive himself, which was the reason of their arriving in this unexpected manner.

Nurse at last had got the children to be what she called
"real bonnie," and indeed, with their fair hair nicely
brushed, their fresh white dresses, their red and blue
sashes (for the twins still stuck to their colours), they
looked quite different creatures to the wild-haired, dirty-
faced little girls in torn brown holland frocks, who had
run along the road half-an-hour before.

Just as they were ready, Aunt Kate appeared to see
why they were so long of coming. When they got to
the drawing-room, they found their uncle and other
aunts and two strangers there. Tommy and the little ones
were already there, also dressed in their best clothes.

"Here are Isabel and Frances," Aunt Kate said, as they
entered. "Go and kiss your mother, dears." Bel and
Fan went up in turn, rather timidly, to a pale, thin lady
in a dark-blue travelling dress, lying on the sofa. Each
received a soft kiss, and stepping back, each was warmly
embraced by a tall brown gentleman with large dark
whiskers.

"How they have grown! Kenneth," sighed their
mamma. "Would you ever have known them? Such wee
tots as they were when they left us! Tommy," rather
sharply, "you will break my chain; you positively must
not pull it like that."

"Come here, my boy," said their father, "come and
play with my charms; you may make ducks and drakes
of them if you like."

"Oh Kenneth, how can you!" remonstrated their mamma; "you know my miniature is among them."

Tommy suddenly drew back the hand he had stretched out towards the charms on his father's watch-guard.

Aunt Margaret here thoughtfully drew away the children's attention by giving them some cake.

"Come here, Isabel," said her mother; and as Bel stood near, she drew her hand through her long hair and continued—"You have really nice hair; if it were properly done and *crêpé*, you would look twice as well."

Bel did not know in the least what *crêpé* meant, but her mother seemed pleased with her, so she felt happy.

"Let me look at you, Frances," then said Mrs Farquhar.

Fan went near to be inspected.

"You have not changed so much; has she, Kenneth? She has still the same little mignon face; something like that picture of your mother," pointing to a portrait on the wall. "But, gracious goodness! how thin the child is! she surely cannot be well?"

"Nothing ever ails her, Charlotte," said Aunt Margaret, warmly. "I don't think there are such healthy children as yours in the parish. Thank God! we never see a doctor."

"Ah! but I don't hold with that at all, Margaret! I think it necessary to see a doctor at least once a week, if it were only to tell you you are well. I always see mine. Why! you might be very ill without knowing it."

B

"That is a very unusual case here," replied Aunt Margaret. "But as the nearest doctor lives twenty miles off, he is only sent for in cases of serious illness."

"But what do you do for headaches and nervous attacks?"

"Oh! we are very seldom troubled with them," said Aunt Margaret, smiling. "Besides, our brother keeps a stock of simple medicines. Experience has given him much skill in their use, and all the sick people in the parish come to consult him."

"What a shocking state of things!" Mrs Farquhar was beginning to exclaim, when nurse appeared to announce that lunch was ready, and to carry off the younger children.

After lunch, Aunt Kate took the twins up to her room, and gave them a little lecture. You want to know what she said, Nina? Well, she told them that they had grown very wild in the last few months, ever since Miss Murray had gone away, and that their mother would be dreadfully shocked if she knew it. "Therefore," she said, "you must try and behave like other children while your parents are there; they do not mean to stay more than a few weeks, as your mother is anxious to visit her own relations."

"Now, you know," continued Aunt Kate, "that Aunt Margaret has a great deal too much to do already, and cannot be expected to look after you. Aunt Isa is not strong enough, and I cannot do it either, so you must just look after yourselves. Try and remember what Miss Murray taught you. By the bye, your mamma is sure to want to hear you play, so you must get up early in the mornings and practise Weber's last waltz; and do, Bel and Fan, give up climbing trees and all these boys' tricks; play quietly near the house, and try and keep your hands and clothes clean. Nurse will always dress you, though she cannot do much more." And then Aunt Kate kissed them, bade them be good girls, and in conclusion, said gravely—

"If you don't behave yourselves, your mother will perhaps send you off to some dreadfully severe school!"

Bel and Fan felt quite frightened. For a day or two, they behaved themselves remarkably well. They got up early, and with a few friendly directions from Aunt Kate, were soon able to play the three first pages of Weber tolerably well. You remember they had never got out the last page.

It was a duet, and they patiently counted one, two, three, under their breaths, in order to keep in time.

But on their playing it before their mother, she remarked, "that there was a total want of delicacy of touch and brilliancy of execution," words which the twins did not understand. She did not, however, seem displeased, and did not ask them to repeat the piece, merely remarking to Aunt Kate, "It was necessary to undergo the ordeal once, but not necessary to repeat it."

But I don't think there is much use in repeating to you what Mrs Farquhar said, for I don't think you would understand it better than Bel and Fan did. They often thought their mother must be using Hindustanee words by mistake.

As I told you, for the first few days the twins behaved admirably—"like lammies," as nurse said. They came in in good time for meals; they were always within call. They played on the lawn or in the orchard; they climbed nothing higher than a wall, and were tolerably neat and clean.

You see they were very much afraid of being sent to school. Having read some silly book about children being badly treated in school, they would do anything to avoid being sent to one.

After a short time, however, more visitors came to Glenmorven, and there being no room at table for the twins, they did not appear in company at lunch. They had always had breakfast and tea in the nursery. Every one's time was so taken up with the visitors, that even nurse had more than usual to do, and the twins were left entirely to themselves. They could not very well help it, perhaps, but they soon ran quite wild again. Their father sometimes came into the nursery, and gave them a hug all round, but they never saw their mother, except in the mornings, when the whole nursery walked into her room to wish her "good morning," and walked out again.

CHAPTER IV.

DID I tell you, Nina, that the twins could ride? They could ride like wild Indians on the rough, shaggy ponies that pastured in Mr Farquhar's fields. They could ride on a gentleman's saddle as well as on a lady's; indeed, they could even manage to hold on bareback.

It had cleared up a little late one evening of a very wet day, and Bel and Fan had gone out. On the road they met the ploughmen on their way to water the horses. The men were leading the big clumsy cart-horses, that had been working all day, to a pond a little way off, where they could drink after their hard toil, and bathe their poor hot legs. The twins often rode the horses to water; so on seeing them, the men stopped as usual and hoisted them up. Bel and Fan liked it very much; they sat on the two front horses, barebacked of course, and holding on by the halters. On nearing the stables they had to pass under some high trees overhanging the road, and in the darkness they suddenly came upon two very bright sparks. Fan's horse shied, that is, jumped suddenly to one side. You see, not being a well-bred horse, accustomed to gentlemen's society, but a clumsy old cart-horse, it did not know that these sparks were cigars, and was frightened. Fan was not frightened, however, but clung bravely to the horse's mane, while the two gentlemen who were smoking rushed forward: one seized the halter, and the other caught Fan and placed her on the ground.

Who do you think the gentlemen were? One was their father, and the other was a Mr Digby Kerr, who, having heard of Colonel Farquhar's arrival, had come to visit him.

Bel had jumped off her horse at once, and both stood now dreadfully ashamed, and expecting their father to scold them. But he only inquired if Fan was hurt, and on finding that she was neither frightened nor hurt, he laughed, pulled her hair, and said they had better run into the house; it was getting too cold and dark for little girls to be out of doors.

" Plenty of pluck there, by Jove, Digby," he said to the young gentleman beside him, when the girls were out of hearing ; " did you ever see such a little monkey? she stuck on like a leech !"

" Fan is plucky," said Digby ; " but I would advise you to keep the matter dark ; the aunts might not like it, and we can give the men a hint not to let them ride again."

So Bel and Fan ran home, sorry for having forgotten their aunt's wishes, but relieved to find their father had not been angry.

Some days after this, all the Glenmorven party had gone across the hill to see a famous view, and to pay some visits; all but Digby Kerr, who preferred having a day's shooting. He was returning after a good day's sport with a well-filled bag, and had reached the avenue, when he heard the children's voices in an adjoining field. He stopped to look at them, but not being able to make out what they were about, leant his gun and bag against one of the poplar trees, and jumped over the low wall.

"Hullo! Bel! what's up?" he called out, as he made his way towards them.

The twins had got hold of a calf. They had put a bridle in its poor soft mouth, and had put a pad or child's saddle on its back. Fan held the calf, while Bel tried with all her strength to fasten the girth or belt of the saddle. You may be sure Digby was much astonished.

"What in all the world are you doing, children?" he asked.

"Oh! we are only going to ride Spotty," Fan calmly answered. "You see Brown Bess and the young mare were put in the carriage; papa is riding Glen, and Bertie, the pony, has wandered off to the very top of the hill, so we had nothing to ride."

"And that lazy Spotty does nothing but eat all day," added Bel, as she tugged at the strap. "It is quite time he should begin to earn his living. He is so fat, too!

he takes as many holes as Bertie. There! it's done at last! Now, Fan, will you get on?"

Digby could not help laughing at the unhappy expression of the poor calf in its experience of earning its bread, but he good-naturedly lifted Fan on its back, while Bel held the bridle.

"I'll lead him a bit," said Bel; "he's much wilder than Glen. I can hardly hold him in—get out of the way, Tommy!"

Tommy was busily engaged in pulling hairs out of the tail of an old cart-horse, that was calmly browsing in the field.

"God bless me, Tommy!" cried Digby, in sudden alarm, "what are you meddling with that horse's tail for? He'll kick you to a certainty!" And he pulled Tommy away.

"Not a bit of him," said Tommy, struggling to get free. "He's used to it; we always get hairs for our fishing-lines that way."

"You are certainly extraordinary children," said Digby, as he let Tommy go.

Meantime the unhappy calf, disliking to have its head uncomfortably tied up, and objecting to the heavy weight on its back, soon broke away from Bel, and went careering about the field. Bel's sharp eye very soon noticed that Fan's seat was not very steady, so she ran after them. Digby followed her example; but before reaching them, the saddle turned, and Fan rolled to the ground! In a moment Digby had reached and picked her up, while Bel caught the rebellious calf, which had slackened its pace on being relieved of its burden.

No! Fan was not hurt, or if she was, she would not confess it. She even wanted to mount Spotty again, but Digby would not let her.

" Well!" said Bel, "I don't think I shall ride him either, stupid thing! We once read in a book, that in some countries oxen were used to draw carts, but I don't think they seem meant for riding on—do you?"

"No, indeed!" said Digby, "and certainly not for young ladies to ride on. Did you ever try Spotty before?"

"Oh, yes!" said Bel; "I had ridden him before papa and mamma came, but it does not seem to have done him any good, stupid thing! That's how it was Fan's turn this time; only, indeed, he behaved worse before, for he threw me into a bed of nettles."

Digby laughed heartily.

" And do you always run about like this?" he asked; "does no one look after you?"

" No; why should they?" returned Bel, who was gene-rally spokeswoman, " we can look after ourselves. We've been so happy ever since Miss Murray went away; oh! so happy, until papa and mamma came."

" How did that spoil your happiness?" asked Digby.

"Oh! we were told we must always behave ourselves;

and we tried to, very hard, for a whole week. But after that more visitors came, and there was no room for us at table, and we became wild and dirty again. Do you know," continued Bel, waxing confidential, "the day papa came, he saw Fan and me in the road, and he asked us to open the gate, and threw us a sixpence. I think he took us for beggars ! "

" Nothing more likely," said Digby, dryly.

" Yes ! but we don't like that ; of course, we like a sixpence well enough, but not when it is thrown at us ; so would you give it back to him ? " continued Bel, producing the piece of money from her pocket. " Don't tell him, of course, that it was us, but just give it back."

Digby with some hesitation took the sixpence, and then helped the twins to carry the saddle to an outhouse.

While hanging it up, he was terribly startled at the report of a gun, suddenly remembering that his was loaded ; and when he got back to the avenue, he found it had been fired off by Tommy. Digby was very angry and much inclined to cuff master Tommy's ears ; but Bel told him that Sandy, the old gamekeeper, often used to let Tommy fire off his gun on his return from shooting.

However, Tommy thought it wise to take himself off, and then Digby, taking up his gun and game-bag, went into the house. That same evening he gave the sixpence back to Colonel Farquhar, who laughed very much at the whole affair, and said he had had a shrewd guess that these little ragged gipsies were his own daughters.

" But for any sake, Digby, don't let her ladyship know of these doings," he said.　By her ladyship he meant Mrs Farquhar.

Digby Kerr was careful not to speak of these, or of several other acts of wildness that took place in the next few days.

CHAPTER V.

BUT as you shall hear, Mrs Farquhar soon saw enough for herself to put the idea of a school into her head. One evening, as she, Aunt Kate, Digby Kerr, and Colonel Farquhar were returning from a drive, Mrs Farquhar's attention was attracted by some objects moving quickly down the hill-side.

On examining them through her glass, she exclaimed—

"Oh! do look, Kenneth! there are two of the natives on wild-looking ponies; they seemed to ride without saddles. How very picturesque! Don't they put you in mind of the donkeys and Arab boys of Cairo?

The Colonel looked up at them, and then exchanged glances with Digby Kerr, while Aunt Kate coloured.

Fortunately, the riders just then disappeared, and the conversation turned to something else.

The truth was, the riders were Bel and Fan. Although Mr Farquhar kept a coachman and groom, besides several men to work on the farm, it was by no means unusual to have great difficulty in finding a man when you wanted one; so the twins had learned by experience, that when they wanted the ponies caught, they must often catch them themselves. They had a variety of ways of catching them, for the ponies were very cunning, and sometimes could not be caught at all, if they were in a rebellious mood. They were just as fond of running wild as the twins themselves were. However, on this occasion they had not been difficult to catch, for the twins had provided themselves with a small basket full of corn. No sooner had the ponies come near and stretched their necks towards the basket, than an active little hand caught each by the mane. In this manner they were quickly secured, the bridles slipt over their heads, and the capture complete.

On reaching the stables they were fortunate in finding the groom there, who saddled the horses for them ; for that was one thing Bel and Fan could not do, they were not strong enough to pull the girths tight.

The carriage-party were still a little way from the house when the twins galloped past them like the wind, their long fair hair flying behind them, and long riding-skirts of their aunts nearly touching their horses' heels. Their mother was horror-struck.

"Isabel! Frances!" she shrieked, "come back! come back!"

But Bel and Fan were already far beyond hearing, and dashed on.

"Kenneth! Kenneth! follow them at once ; they'll be thrown off! they'll be disfigured for life!" screamed Mrs Farquhar.

"Calm yourself, for Heaven's sake! Charlotte," implored Colonel Farquhar; "there is not the least occasion for fear."

"I assure you there is not, dear Charlotte," added Aunt Kate; "the girls are quite accustomed to the ponies, and ride almost every day."

"·Did you notice how well they sit, Farquhar?" said Digby Kerr; "a year's riding-school could not improve them. By Jove! Mrs Farquhar, if they live to go out to India, you will be very proud of the graceful and daring riding of your daughters a few years hence."

"Indeed, mem, ye needna be frighted," put in the old coachman, who had pulled up at the first alarm, and was listening to the conversation. "The young leddies are grand riders; it was myself teached them, and they can ride just as well without a saddle as with one."

The carriage now drove on, Mrs Farquhar being relieved from her fear for the girls' safety; but the coachman's remark awoke a suspicion in her mind, that the "picturesque natives" had been none other than her own daughters; and for the first time she began to think whether she should not remove them from Glenmorven.

What curious noise is that, Nina? Oh! only Bertie snoring! Well, my story is becoming rather long; it is no wonder the little fellow has fallen asleep.

Still more visitors arrived, and the house became so full that even the twins were turned out of their little room, and had to sleep in the nursery. Among the guests was the Honourable Mrs Seton, a great friend of their mother's. She brought a maid, and the maid must have a room, and thus the twins had to turn out.

They were rather unhappy in these days. They never could get any rides now, for the horses were always busy, being used to convey the guests on all sorts of expeditions. They felt themselves always in the way, whether indoors or out; indeed, Aunt Kate had told them that the best thing they could do would be to keep as much out of sight as possible. Therefore they did not feel very sorry when they heard that their parents intended to leave in a few days.

Indeed, I am afraid that they rather looked forward to their departure as a relief, although they were really fond of their father, and admired their mother, for she always wore such lovely dresses and sparkling jewels.

Two days before that fixed for Colonel and Mrs Farquhar's departure, as it was a fine warm evening, it was proposed that the company should stroll by the banks of the river, where the sweet smelling hay was being made in the grassy meadows. They soon broke into groups, and Mrs Seton and Mrs Farquhar found themselves together.

"This is really a heavenly evening! Leonora," said Mrs Farquhar; "had we a regimental band to amuse us, it would be perfection."

"It would be a little more lively, certainly," said Mrs Seton. "This is really a lovely place to spend a few summer weeks in; but I cannot understand how Mr Farquhar and his sisters can exist here always."

"Nor can I," answered Mrs Farquhar. "I should be bored to death! I hope Kenneth will not insist on my accompanying him, when he returns for the longer visit he speaks of."

"While your children are here, Charlotte, I should think you would wish to return."

"Oh, Leonora! I wished so much to speak to you about my girls. Kenneth won't let me find fault with his sisters; but I must say that the *maintien* of Isabel and Frances has been shamefully neglected."

While conversing, the ladies had arrived at the banks of a stream that ran across the path into the river. It was the "burn" that ran down the hillside. Though now only a streamlet, in winter it was quite a torrent, and had cut deeply into the sandy terrace, so that its banks near the river were many feet high. It too had its little grassy meadow in the summer time, and this place was one of the twins' favourite play-grounds. They had built a little hut against one of the steep banks, and here they often played at keeping house.

Near the hut a peat-fire was now burning, over which a childish figure was bending. A few paces off, another child was washing some objects, which looked like potatoes in the stream. When she came in sight of this scene, Mrs Farquhar had recourse, as usual, to her eye-glass.

" Look here, Leonora! here is something very interesting, I declare! I think it must be a gipsy encampment. I did not know before that gipsies wandered so far north."

On examining the supposed gipsies more closely, an unpleasant suspicion entered her mind, and she would gladly have turned away. But too late! for the child at the fire raised her head, and displayed the fair hair and very grimy face of Bel.

" Heavens! Isabel," cried her mother, " what a fright you are! What on earth are you doing here?"

Bel stood up very much frightened and startled, and half inclined to run away.

" I am only roasting potatoes," she stammered, " and Fan is washing them."

Mrs Farquhar turned pale. Mrs Seton laughed good-naturedly. Fan had also stood up, letting her potatoes roll into the stream.

" There, Leonora!" exclaimed Mrs Farquhar, pathetically; " you see what training the children are getting here."

" Oh! I assure you I don't feel the least shocked," said Mrs Seton. " When my sisters and I were young, in Ireland, we used to play about just the same. A year or two at Madame Savan's will soon put all that to rights."

The ladies then left the children, and resumed their walk and conversation, Mrs Seton supplying Mrs Farquhar with all particulars about Madame Savan's school.

When the ladies were gone, Bel and Fan returned to their potatoes, but Bel's had burnt to cinders, and Fan's had been carried away by the stream. So their little feast was spoilt.

Next forenoon the twins were sent for, to go to their mamma's room. They felt rather frightened, but they need not have been, for their mamma sent for them in order to give them some pretty presents she had selected for them out of a box of things she had brought from India—sweet sandalwood fans, and baskets, and some ivory toys. She told them she had brought some trinkets for them, and some more fine dresses, but these she would not now give them, as they would be thrown away at Glenmorven. The twins were delighted with the fans and baskets, and they spent a great part of the rest of the day in sniffing them, to enjoy the sweet smell.

CHAPTER VI.

NEXT morning every one was up very early, to be in time for the steamer. Mrs Seton and her maid were also going by her, so there was quite a large party to convey to the shore. The Farquhars always went so far with their parting guests, to see that they got safely on board the steamer.

You think it easy to get on board a steamer, Nina!

No doubt it is, when one has only to walk on board from a pier. But at Glenmorven there was no pier, and people had to be taken out to the steamer in a boat; and in stormy weather, it was both unpleasant and. dangerous. However, on this occasion the sea was smooth. The twins had also gone to the shore, and could not help shedding a few tears as they watched the boat that conveyed their parents to the steamer. But their tears soon dried, and when at last they saw the steamer fairly disappear, they seemed to feel happier than they had done for a long time.

Now they could play how and where they liked; now they could ride whenever they felt inclined; now they could climb trees again; now they would not require to be always trying to keep out of sight, nor be forced to slip in and out by the back entrance, feeling as if they were culprits ! Now they would feel at home again at Glenmorven, as they had done for so many years.

For the next week or two they were indeed perfectly happy. All their old liberty was restored ; and to make up for their late discomfort, their uncle and aunts indulged them in every way. It is possible their aunts may have had some idea of what, Nina, I daresay you may be beginning to suspect was going to happen. But the twins thought the danger was past ; and had indeed forgotten it.

Their surprise and distress, therefore, were great when, one unhappy day, a letter came from their mamma to say that she thought Isabel and Frances were too old for a governess, and would be better at school ; that she had found an admirable school for them at Brighton ; that she had already arranged with Madame Savan that they should go there at once. She wished them, therefore, to start for the South by the first steamer, under the care of a servant ; unless, indeed, their Aunt Kate, who had promised to pay her a visit, could come now and take charge of them. She herself would meet them in London, and get their necessary outfit before going on to school.

Mrs Farquhar had all this so well arranged, that the only matter to be discussed was, whether Aunt Kate could possibly go on so short a notice. But seeing the despair depicted in the faces of the twins, who were quite unable to speak, Aunt Kate resolved to go; for she could not bear to think of letting them go alone so far, and to strangers.

Poor Fan! poor Bel! so this was the end of it all! For this they had rebelled against Miss Murray!

Were children ever so unfortunate? All they wanted was to be let alone; and now they were to be sent off to a hateful school, to learn music and languages, and stuff of that sort, whether they would or no!

It was at breakfast time that this dreadful letter was read, and as soon as possible the twins slipt out into the garden. They went down to the far corner of the orchard and got up into a pear tree. This tree was called the umbrella tree, because the lower branches were thick and strong near the trunk, and formed delightful seats, while the upper branches drooped and hid any one who might be sitting there. Here Bel and Fan recovered their speech and began their lamentations.

"Oh, dear! oh, dear!" cried Bel, "it is too cruel of mamma to take us away. Why couldn't she leave us here?"

"Oh! what shall we do?" sobbed Fan; "it will be much worse than having a governess; oh, I wish we had been good when Miss Murray was here!"

"Oh! why couldn't mamma have remained in India?" exclaimed Bel; "she was happy there, and we were happy here; oh, dear! oh, dear!"

" But we won't go ! " said Fan; " we'll run away first! "

" If we could only miss the steamer," cried the practical Bel, " that would give us a week longer here. Let us think of some place."

"Oh, Bel! I'm ready to do anything. Let us run away to the hills, where nobody can find us."

" But we might die of hunger, Fan ; and our bodies would be found like the babes in the wood. No ; we could not do that."

" Well, let us go off in the boat to old Rory, who lives on the Island ; I am sure he would hide us and give us food."

" Yes, I am sure he would ; but do you think we could row so far ? Besides, Fan, the people on the shore would see us, and tell where we had gone."

" Well," said Fan, after a pause, " I can think of nothing else, unless we go to the Big Cave."

"That's the very thing, Fan; we'll go to the Big Cave ; they'll never be able to find us there, and I think we had better just set off at once and look at it."

So the pair came down from the tree and set off up the hill. The cave was pretty far off, and rather difficult to find ; for a number of large stones had fallen down from a steep cliff above it, and nearly hidden the entrance— one of them indeed had almost blocked it up. The children had been there but once before, and had not then examined it attentively ; great, therefore, was their disappointment when they at last discovered it, to find it quite different from what they had expected.

Its sides were dripping with water, and a little stream ran through the middle of its floor. They felt certain there must be lizards there, if not even serpents.

No; it would not do at all to hide in, even for a few hours. They must think of some other plan.

Down the hill they slowly came, in a very melancholy state of mind.

On the hillside, a little way above the stables, was a large sheep-pen or "fank." Near this stood a ruinous hut or bothy, used by the men who watched the sheep, when they were gathered for shearing or other purposes. When the twins came to this hut, they stood still and looked at one another.

" I declare, Fan," said Bel, " here is just the very place we want! Let us go in and examine it."

On going in they found the floor was clean and dry, and there was a heap of straw in one corner. The door indeed was rather off the hinges, and of the original two small panes of glass in the window, but part of one remained; but the hardy twins found the place delightful, and made up their minds at once that it would do.

So now, my dears, we have come at last to the " Camping Out." The twins resolved to hide themselves here the night before the steamer sailed, and not make their appearance until they were sure she was gone, and thus gain a week's respite.

As they had read Miss Edgeworth's *Barring Out,*— you have read it too, Nina,—and remembered how the boys supplied themselves beforehand with provisions and other things, they resolved to do the same, and to begin at once to lay in their stores.

They became quite cheerful over their project, and as soon as they got to the house they went at once to the pantry and removed all the candle ends they could find in the bedroom candlesticks. They then went to their hut near the river, where they had a box of matches, an old frying-pan, and some other little things that might be useful ; but they did not dare to return to the hut that day, for fear of attracting notice.

They had no difficulty, in the course of the next few days, in collecting provisions. Some oat-cake and some meal they easily got from the cook, as they were in the habit of coming to her for food for their pets. There was always a large quantity of potatoes kept in an open out-house, so they easily secured a basketful of them. Sticks and peats were not forgotten. Indeed, so occupied and happy did they appear, that Aunt Margaret could not help feeling a little hurt at it, and remarked, "that the twins had not very warm hearts, after all, or they could not be so cheerful at parting from what had so long been their home."

I daresay you are wondering all this time what has become of Tommy, that he is never mentioned, and that he did not find out what the twins were about.

Well; soon after his parents' arrival, Tommy had been sent to the parish school. It was a very good one, and what between being there all day, and having a number of lessons to prepare in the evenings, with which Aunt Isa helped him, he saw very little of the girls.

At last, the last day before the steamer sailed, arrived. Bel and Fan had finished all their preparations, and they felt restless and anxious, and kept wandering about. They went to their aunts' sitting-room and found them busy helping Aunt Kate to make up warm cloaks for the travellers. As soon as they got in, Aunt Kate called out, " Now children! do keep away; don't you see how busy we all are." So they went up-stairs to the nursery and kissed and said good-bye to the children, for they felt that they might not see them for some days. Then they wandered out again, but felt no inclination for their usual plays, and resolved at last to go and see the horses. They found the ponies were quite near the house.

" Fan," said Bel, " I think it would be very nice to have a last ride after tea."

" I think so too, Bel, and then, perhaps, we would not feel so dull."

So at tea time they told nurse they were going after tea to have a ride up the glen. During tea, when nurse was not looking, they kept putting bread and butter into their pockets, until at last nurse, who was angry at having to go down-stairs to fetch more, began to scold, and said, " They were mair like greedy gledds than young leddies, and they would have to mend their mainers when they went to schule."

When tying on their riding-skirts, and making ready to leave, they felt a strong wish to go and kiss their uncle and aunts, for they began to feel quite low-spirited and disinclined to carry out their plan; but their spirits revived when they once got on the ponies, and found themselves cantering up the glen. The evening was very hot and still, and it soon began to grow dark. The twins thought it was time to return, so they rode back slowly, and at some distance from the stables dismounted, and led the ponies up the hill in the direction of the hut. On reaching it, they unsaddled and unbridled the horses, and turned them loose upon the hill. The saddles, Bel said, would make excellent pillows, and the skirts would do for blankets. It had become so dark, that they had to feel their way inside the hut to the corner where the straw was. Here they sat down, hardly daring to speak or breathe for fear of being overheard.

CHAPTER VII.

AFTER a time, hearing no sound but the noise of the burn, they grew a little bolder. It was very tiresome sitting there in the dark, so they thought they might as well lie down. They arranged the saddles to put their heads on, lay down on the straw, and spread the riding-skirts over them.

As they were lying down, Fan said—

"Don't you think, Bel, we might eat some of our bread and butter? I am very hungry, for I hardly ate a bite at tea?"

"Oh, no!" said the prudent Bel, "we must not begin to eat so soon; you see, we may have to stay here for a day or two; sometimes the steamer is a day late."

Fan lay quiet for a while, and then she began again. "Oh! Bel, I wish we might light a candle, it is so very dark."

"We dare not light one yet, for fear any one should see the light of it; but when it gets later we can do it. Here, if you are frightened, lie quite close to me, and we can then put one skirt over the other, which will be warmer."

"Oh, dear! how hard the saddle feels," was Fan's next remark.

"Well, I expected they would have made better pillows," Bel confessed.

Both were silent for a time, till Fan called out suddenly and hysterically—

"Bel! Bel! what noise is that?"

They both sat up and listened, but found that it was only rain pattering on the roof. The night had quite changed, and it now rained heavily.

They lay down again. "Bel!" said Fan, after a pause, "what if mad Christopher should come across the hill and should come in here? You know nurse often told us we should be sure to meet him if we ran about on the hills."

"But we never did meet him," said Bel calmly, "and nurse only said that to frighten us, and to keep us from going too far away. But I really think, Fan, that we might light one of our candles now," she continued; "it is such a bad night, I am sure no one will be out, and I think we might eat some of our bread and butter too."

Fan quite rallied at hearing this. Bel got up and groped about until she found the match-box and a piece of candle. The first two or three matches she lit went out, but Fan held up a skirt to screen off the draught, and then a match burned long enough to light the candle. When it was lit, they discovered that with all their forethought, they had forgotten to provide any kind of candle-stick. However, at last they managed to fix the piece of candle on a projecting stone in the rough wall ; and then Bel hung up one of the skirts over the window, to make all safe. After this, they shared the bread and butter that was in Fan's pocket, and when they had eaten it they felt much better, and arranged to lie down again.

They felt, too, that they were really heroines, spending a night alone in this lonely hut. They had actually begun to doze, and had forgotten the hardness of the saddles, when Bel suddenly started up, saying that some-thing cold had touched her hand. Bel had strong nerves, and was not a bit afraid of ghosts ; but she had heard of pole-cats that came to steal the chickens, and she thought that this must have been the nose of one.

The candle was just going out, so she got up to light another. "Oh ! dear me, what shall we do when the candles are done?" she said. "The draught makes them run down at once." Bel had hardly lain down again, when she felt a cold drop on her face, and discovered that the rain had soaked through the roof, and was dropping down upon their bed.

So they were obliged to get up and drag the straw, saddles and all, to another corner of the hut.

After their bed was arranged, they lay down again, but not to sleep. Poor thin Fan was shivering with cold, and they had now but one skirt to cover themselves with. Each by this time had secretly resolved that she would not pass such another cold wakeful night in the bothy, but go back sometime to-morrow, making sure first, of course, that the steamer had sailed.

They began to be very miserable, for sleep was impossible. Fan felt inclined to cry, and Bel tried to comfort her.

" If we can only manage to stay here till the steamer sails, it will be all right, and I am sure it must be near morning now, Fan ; and besides, I am sure you would not like to go home when it is dark."

"Oh ! no, no," said Fan, with a sob. " We might meet mad Christopher, you know."

At that moment there was a loud knock at the door.

"Oh ! it's mad Christopher ; he'll kill us, he'll murder us !" shrieked Fan, crouching up into the corner.

Bel, losing all presence of mind, began screaming too.

The door was pushed violently open. The girls covered their faces, and shrieked with terror.

" Bel ! Fan ! my poor children," said a kind voice they knew ; and, looking up, the twins saw their uncle, dripping with rain from head to foot, even his grey hair quite wet.

" Don't be frightened, dears," he continued ; "you see it is your old uncle. Thank God ! you are safe," he added gravely.

"Oh, uncle ! we were so frightened, we thought it was

mad Christopher ; we'll never, never, do so again," they both cried, getting up and running to him, and clinging to his wet coat. He kissed them warmly, and then said, "Remain here for a minute, dears," and went to the door. Here he shouted to some one at a short distance, and then returned, followed by the coachman carrying a lantern and some shawls.

"Here, children, wrap yourselves well up in these warm shawls."

Bel was rather frightened when she saw how very white Fan looked and how she shivered ; but she shook just as much herself, though she was not quite so pale.

"What are those things in the corner?" asked their uncle. "Oh! saddles are they? Well, they and the riding-skirts are safe enough here till to-morrow. But it was fortunate for you, girls, that when you covered the window you forgot to do so to the door, for it was the light shining through the chinks of it that guided me here. Now, Fan, I am going to carry you home, and the coachman can carry Bel."

The repentant girls were carried through the rain to the farm-yard, where their uncle stopped an instant to leave word that they had been found (for all the Glenmorven people were afoot, seeking them on the hills or by the river), and then they proceeded to the house.

Not a word of reproach did their kind uncle utter for all the trouble and anxiety they had caused him ; from the time nurse had announced in an excited manner, "that it was far past ten o'clock, and that the twins had not come home." Bel and Fan could have borne scoldings and reproaches; indeed, had quite expected them; but this kindness and forbearance quite overcame them, and filled them with remorse.

"Oh! uncle, uncle, can you forgive us? we are so sorry," sobbed Fan, as he carried her along.

"Of course I can, dear; don't distress yourself so much. I am only too thankful to have found you. It was a little mistake, and I see that you are very sorry for it."

Fan only cried the more at this, and thought—Oh, what a kind uncle! and if he gets cold and dies, it will be all our fault.

As they neared the house, they met some of the servants anxious for news; and in the hall their aunts and nurse were waiting to receive them. Aunt Margaret took Fan out of Mr Farquhar's arms, and nurse took charge of Bel. Their aunts said nothing on their appearance, but nurse, with less self-control, called out—

"There they are at last, the tawpies! rinnin' awa frae hame, and garrin' everybody lose their night's rest. And the maister's fair drooket, and—"

"Hush, hush, nurse, that's enough," said Mr Farquhar. "It is not scolding we want now, but some hot tea. You had better go and get it ready, and see that hot-water bottles are put in the children's beds directly."

Their aunts took the twins into the warm parlour, took off their shawls, and kissed and embraced them tearfully. If they had felt rather inclined to scold them, the pale and tear-stained faces of the children prevented their doing it. Aunt Margaret then went to her brother's room to see that there was a good fire there, and that he quickly put off his wet clothes; while Aunt Kate helped the twins to some hot tea that nurse had just brought in. After this Aunt Kate went with them to their room to see them quickly into bed; and while helping to undress them, she told them of the dreadful alarm they had all been in, quite believing at last that some terrible accident must have happened to them. Bel and Fan began again to cry at this, and wondered very much how it was that they had never thought of the distress their disappearance would cause their uncle and aunts. You are crying, too, Nina, I see. All this trouble came from the twins trying to avoid obeying their mamma's orders, and forgetting what they had been often taught to repeat— " Honour thy father and thy mother "—which just means, "obey your parents;" so I hope you will take a lesson from it. Aunt Kate then kissed them, and said " good-night;" and they were not many minutes in their warm beds (oh ! so different from the damp straw and the hard saddles) when they fell sound asleep; so sound, indeed, that it was with difficulty and a good deal of shaking that nurse got them wakened at six o'clock next morning.

But though they felt very stiff and sleepy, remembering last night they were determined to be very good to-day ; so they got up at once, were quickly dressed, breakfasted, and ready to set off for the shore. All the people about the place had come to bid them good-bye, and when they got to the village the people there were all standing at their doors for the same purpose. A little crowd even followed them down to the shore where the boat was waiting. Their warm new cloaks were tied on, Aunt Margaret kissed them (Aunt Isa had been some days confined to the house, and they had said good-bye to her in her room). Their uncle lifted them into the boat, helped Aunt Kate in, and then followed himself to see them all right on board the steamer. In all this haste and excitement, the children were fairly off almost before they knew it ; and on board the steamer were so many new sights and sounds, that they almost forgot that they were leaving dear Glenmorven, with all its delights, far behind.

THE BONFIRE.

CHAPTER I.

TEN months have passed; the school at Brighton, where the twins have been receiving their education, is closed for the summer holidays, and all the pupils are dispersed here and there to their different homes. School had not been such a disagreeable place as the twins expected it to be. At first they had felt very much out of place among so many strangers, had been careless about learning their lessons, had often spoilt their eyes with crying, and had wasted much of their time in longing for Glenmorven.

The result was, that they were always at the bottom of their classes, and in disgrace with their governesses and masters. One day Madame Savan spoke to them on the subject, and told them how much disappointed their parents would be if they did not make better progress in their studies.

This had a good effect; and being naturally clever,

they no sooner began to exert themselves than they generally rose in their classes. After a time they began to find a certain pleasure and excitement in school life, and to obtain a prize became their highest ambition. They had their friendships with some of the girls, and quarrels with others, as school girls always have ; they felt pleased when their masters praised them ; they listened with interest to the accounts the older girls gave of the delights of the breaking-up party.

The twins are now on their way to Glenmorven, and the steamer has nearly reached the bay. Bel and Fan look very smart—they wear long high-heeled boots with tassels, panniers to their dresses, and their long fair hair plaited in two tails, according to the newest fashion.

It was perhaps a good thing that Madame Savan could not see them on their arrival at Glenmorven, for I am afraid she would have felt very much shocked, and believed that her lectures on lady-like behaviour, and so on, had been thrown away.

Even the fine English accent they had acquired seemed to leave them directly they caught sight of their uncle, Aunt Margaret, old Rory, and the other natives waiting for them on the shore, the evening of their arrival, and they fell at once into their old Highland singing tone.

"God bless you, dears," said their uncle, kissing each affectionately as he helped them out of the boat.

" My darlings, how you have grown !" cried Aunt

Margaret, as she kissed them repeatedly while they clung to her neck. "You are quite grown-up young ladies."

"Oh! no, no, Aunt Margaret, we are just the same," said Bel.

"Oh! darling Aunt Margaret, how happy we are to be here again," cried Fan, repeating the embraces.

And then they both ran to shake hands with old Rory and their other particular friends among the little crowd of onlookers.

"Come here, Bel," cried their uncle, "and see if your luggage is all right. I am very glad to see you looking so well, dear children," he continued ; "Brighton seems to have agreed with you."

"Oh yes!" said Bel, "we like Brighton well enough, but it is not like dear Glenmorven."

"I think we had better hasten home now," said Aunt Margaret ; "the carriage has been waiting some time, and you must be hungry."

"Oh!" cried Fan, as they got into the carriage, "there are Brown Bess and the old mare again! Oh, you darlings."

"How are Glen, and Bertie the pony, Aunt Margaret?" asked Bel.

"Oh! you ridiculous children," laughed Aunt Margaret, "to ask for the horses before you have asked for your brothers and sisters!"

"We know they are well, because you always wrote us

about them," said Bel ; " but no one ever wrote about
the horses.   But why didn't Tommy come to meet us ? "

" He was not at hand when we left home ; but I daresay he is not far off, for by this time he must have
noticed the smoke of the steamer."

Just as Aunt Margaret supposed, at the next turning
they met Tommy, very red and hot with running.   The
twins made room for him beside them.   At first he was a
little shy of such smart young ladies ; but he was soon
at his ease, and had a great deal to tell about the horses
—how Glen had been shod that morning, and how
Bertie, the pony, was growing too fat and lazy, all because he was not allowed to ride him enough (with
an injured look at Aunt Margaret).   At the gate Aunt
Isa and the children were waiting, where there was
more hugging and kissing.   Nurse too was not far off, and
delighted to see her " bonnie bairns grown into sic braw
young leddies."   She was particularly delighted with
their dresses, but looked doubtfully at the long tails of
hair.

How good everything tasted to the twins at tea that
first night !   They were sure they had never tasted such
delicious food ! chops so tender ! butter so delicate ! tea
so refreshing ! scones so crumby ! jam so sweet !

After tea they wanted to have a ride, but Aunt Margaret said they had had quite enough of excitement for
one day, and must go soon and quietly to bed.

Aunt Kate was from home when they arrived, on a visit to her friends, the Browns, who had shootings in the neighbourhood.

On their leaving school, Madame Savan had told the twins that she had been much pleased with their conduct during the last half session, and that she had been able to send a very good report of them to their mamma (now returned to India). She believed, if they worked hard, they would be sure of prizes next session ; but she advised them to keep up their music and French during the holidays, by at least two hours' daily study. Madame evidently knew nothing of Glenmorven, or she might have spared them this advice.

If nurse thought that school had changed the "daft tawpies" into "wiselike young leddies," she was much mistaken. They had not been a week at Glenmorven when they were as wild as ever. Tommy had holidays too, and being a year older now, was able to go about more with them than he had done the year before.

Many a sigh did nurse give over the fashionably cut dresses, torn or dirty ; over the beautiful tall boots, with their dozen buttons and silk tassels, scratched and muddy.

At last, to stop her constant scolding, the twins hunted out some old holland frocks, and began to wear them, only consenting to put on their new dresses when visitors were expected.

So, to see them running about, they were exactly the untidy figures of last year—only still more ridiculous—as their frocks were far too short for them. But, after all, their appearance did not matter much, for ah! they were so happy.

CHAPTER II.

ABOUT a quarter of a mile nearer the sea than Glenmorven House, the river made a bend, which took it close to the high road. Here the stream was divided by an island, a pretty grassy island, with one tree growing in state in the middle of it. The island was not in the middle of the river, but much nearer the bank on one side. On this side the stream was narrow, but on the other it was broad and shallow.

Before the twins returned, Tommy had often lain on the bank of the narrow channel and watched the darting trout and gliding eels that were passing up and down it. He had often wished to make an eel trap, but could not hit upon a plan.

This desire and difficulty he confided to the twins; so after a survey of the spot, and much consultation, they decided upon making the channel still narrower by filling up its sides with stones, and then fastening a sort of bag net across it. This work, of course, took up a good many days, and when the channel was narrow enough for their purpose, they got a piece of net from old Rory, the fisherman.

At last all was ready, the net was fastened to a stout

string, a biggish stone was placed on one end of the string on the bank, and Tommy held the other end in his hand, ready to pull the net on shore, when any fish should be in it. It is a beautiful afternoon, Bel and Fan are with Tommy on the island, watching the eel trap with great interest. Bel lies lazily on the short grass, sweet with white clover and purple thyme, while Fan is helping Tommy to adjust the net. The stream is so narrow that one can easily step across it now. When the net is fastened, Fan sits down beside Bel, and Tommy lies down on the very edge of the stream ; he holds one end of the string ready to pull up the net, and peers into the water.

"I wouldn't sit so near the edge, Tommy, if I were you," said Bel ; "the eels will see your shadow, and turn back."

"How can they?" said Tommy ; "uncle said they were blind."

"Oh no!" said Bel; "uncle said they were deaf. They have eyes, stupid boy! and see as well as you do."

"Very well then," said Tom, moving about half an inch away, "I'm sure they can't see me now; but if I don't see them, how shall I know when to pull up the net?"

"What a lot of smoke is in the bay!" said Fan. "I think it must be Mr Brown's steam launch. I know Aunt Kate was expected home to-day."

"Oh bother!" said Tom; "if Mr Brown comes he will spoil all our fun."

"I say, do you remember Uncle Charles, Fan?" asked Bel after a short silence, during which all eyes had been fixed upon the net.

"No; I don't remember him very well, but I think he must be like papa; and then he is sure to be very nice."

"Oh! but he is only a little older than Aunt Kate, so he cannot be like papa," said Bel; "but he must be nice too: he sent us such pretty books at Christmas."

"I wonder if he will bring us any this time. Some picture-books would be very nice for wet weather, or when nurse dresses us up for visitors."

"He might bring me a real gun, or a fishing-rod, I don't mind much which," said Tom; "but," added he provokingly, "perhaps he may be like Mr Brown."

"Oh! if I thought that," said Bel, "I would not wish him to come at all."

"Look out, girls!" shouted Tom suddenly, pulling the string sharply, and flinging the net high and dry on the grass. Some creatures were no doubt wriggling within it, and the girls flew to catch the slippery prey, and put them in a small tin pail of water they had brought for the purpose. But when they seized the eels they wriggled so, that they screamed and let them go.

"What fools you girls are!" cried Tom indignantly, catching up one larger than the others. But he had hardly grasped it, when he gave a cry and let it fall, declaring it had bitten him.

Only one eel, and that a very tiny one, reached the pail; all the others wriggled themselves in a few moments back into the water.

" Did the eel give you a bad bite?" asked Bel, coming to examine Tommy's hand, but finding no mark.

" One can be very much hurt without a mark," declared Tommy. " I tell you it nipped my finger when I caught it up; though of course you won't believe it, as it does not bleed. But it feels better now certainly."

" Oh, I daresay it will soon be quite well," said Bel pointedly.

" I'll tell you what," said Fan, "we'll catch them next time in our handkerchiefs; and I'll get mine ready," producing, as she spoke, a remarkably dirty rag from her pocket.

Tommy set the net again, and the girls sat on the grass a little way off, and resumed their conversation.

" Look here, girls," said Tommy. " Sandy was telling me the other day, that when uncle was young, and used to go to college, on his return they always lighted a bonfire on the Dun, to welcome him home. Would it not be fun to make a bonfire when Uncle Charles comes; you know he has not been here for a long time?"

" Oh yes! that would be delightful," cried Fan. "Oh!

what fun making a bonfire would be; and I am sure
Uncle Charles would be pleased."

"I think we must ask uncle's leave first," said Bel;
"and then we must ask Sandy to help us, and show us
how to make it."

"I know a place where there are lots of dry sticks,"
said Tom; "heaps and heaps of them."

They sat a while silent after this, and Fan wandered to
the tree, and climbed up a little way, until she was high
enough to overlook the road leading from the village.

"I declare, there they come!" exclaimed Fan. "Aunt
Kate, Miss Brown, and Mr Brown."

"Are you quite sure?" asked Bel. "Let me have a
look too," and she ran to the tree.

Yes; there was no doubt about it. There was Mr
Brown's white hat; and there was Aunt Kate's pink sun-
shade, that she used to wear last summer.

"Now, what shall we do?" asked Bel. "If we stay
here, Mr Brown will be sure to come down to us, and
poke at our net. The others might perhaps not notice
us; but nothing escapes that opera-glass of his, that he
always carries about with him."

"Besides," said Fan, "I would not like Aunt Kate to
see us while we are so untidy. Nurse told us to be sure
to be home in time to be dressed."

"I think, if we make haste," said Bel, "we can get
home before them; but we must be quick"

"Oh, stop, stop!" cried Tom; "there's such a big eel coming this way. Oh! such a monster! If you would only wait a minute, I would be sure to catch him."

"Never mind him," said Bel, "unless you want Mr Brown to come down and help you to catch him."

"Pull up the net, and get what you can," advised Fan.

"Why do you speak so loud!" cried Tom crossly; "you have frightened the monster eel away. Well, here goes," he said, pulling up the net; "our fun is spoilt, of course."

This time they succeeded in securing a couple of small eels, popped them into the pail, put on the lid, and set off towards the road.

CHAPTER III.

BETWEEN them and the road was a bank, thickly covered with high ferns. The children had delayed their departure too long, and finding they could not reach the road unobserved, they crouched down among the ferns, until Mr Brown and the ladies should pass.

Presently, from their hiding-place, they saw Mr Brown passing along the road, walking between Aunt Kate and his sister. They all looked rather hot and dusty; the ladies had parasols up, and Mr Brown carried Aunt Kate's sketch-book. On they went up the road, until they came near to where it took a turn out of sight.

There they all stopped, and began to talk eagerly; Mr Brown insisting on doing something, which the ladies evidently wished to prevent. Something had been lost or forgotten, and he wanted to go back for it. In the end, he turned back, while the ladies went on towards Glenmorven House.

Now, children, I know you must agree with me, that what the Glenmorven children did next was very naughty and ill-bred; but they did dislike Mr Brown, and it was Tommy who began it.

Mr Brown had just past their hiding-place, when Tommy raised his head cautiously, and cried in a fine voice, "Mr Brown! Edward!" then popped down again.

Mr Brown paused, looked all round, and then went on.

Bel now raised up her head, and exclaimed, " Edward! Edward! Ned!"

Mr Brown turned round, and though he was hot and tired, he hurried back after the ladies, thinking they had called him ; though he knew it was not his sister's voice, and he thought it strange Miss Kate should call him by his Christian name.

Tom and the twins were still in their hiding-place, when they saw him hastening down the road again, looking very red and angry ; for the ladies had denied having called him.   Miss Kate had laughed at him, and he was dreadfully put out.

He had barely passed the spot where the children were, when again the cry came on his ear, " Edward! Ned! dear Neddy!"

He turned round this time quickly, too quick for Fan, whose fair hair he saw among the ferns.   However, he took no notice, but proceeded down the road.

"What a lark!" cried Tom, when Mr Brown was out of sight. " Didn't he look mad, and as red as the turkey cock, when it is in a rage? You did it very well, girls!"

" What business has he to be always going about with Aunt Kate?" said Fan indignantly. "I suppose he thought she was calling him just now."

" Young ladies like gentlemen to go about with them," said Bel with gravity. "When you are grown up, Fan, you'll like it too."

" Indeed I won't," said Fan; "or, if I do, it will be some one like Digby Kerr, with a brown face and a gold watch, and—"

" Mr Brown has a gold watch twice as big as Digby Kerr's," interrupted Tom.

" Oh yes, I know," cried Fan; "but Mr Brown has such a lot of whiskers, and such white hands!"

" And such a soft voice," said Bel. "I can't—"

But Bel never finished her sentence, for there stood Mr Brown himself, with a very red face in the midst of his whiskers. In one hand he held Aunt Kate's handkerchief, which was what he had gone to look for; in the other, a slight switch.

" Now, children, which shall I begin with? for I mean to cane Tom, and to kiss you girls," at the same time giving Tom a few slight cuts across the legs.

The twins gave a frightful shriek at this threat.

Fan caught hold of Bel; they lost their footing, and rolled down the little bank; while Tom ran off as fast as he could, using some naughty names, I am afraid, to Mr Brown. The twins soon picked themselves up, and also took to their heels ; and Mr Brown, soon seeing he had no chance of catching them, went back to find Aunt Kate's handkerchief, which had been again dropped. He found it close to a pail of water of the children's, which had been upset over it ; but Mr Brown did not mind its being wet, picked it up, and put it in his pocket.

When he was fairly gone, Tom and the twins returned to the spot where they had left the pail, found it empty, and did not thank Mr Brown for causing the loss of their eels.

After dinner, in the drawing-room, Mr Brown pulled out the handkerchief he had taken so much trouble to find, and handed it with a pretty speech to Miss Kate. What was his dismay to see her jump up, and with a cry throw it away ! He had not alone presented her with a very wet handkerchief, but also with a very lively eel, which wriggled about on the carpet. The ladies shrieked, Mr Brown seized the tongs, and tried in vain to catch the eel.

Aunt Margaret hurried into the room to see what the noise was about, and not having such delicate nerves, boldly caught the eel in her handkerchief, and threw it out of the window. Mr Brown thought, of course, that this was another trick the children had played him ; but we know it was quite an accident.

But we must confess that when the children heard of

it afterwards, they were quite delighted, and thought it served Mr Brown right for teasing them, quite forgetting that they had on this occasion first teased him.

It would be difficult to give the exact reason why they had such a dislike to Mr Brown. It was very silly of them, because we should never dislike people without good cause. They would perhaps have said, it was because he was English ; but then Digby Kerr, whom they liked very much, was half English ; and the twins had many friends among the Brighton girls, who were out and out English.

He perhaps took too much pains to please them, for he was a good-hearted young man, fond of children. He used to follow them about, give them advice, and interfere with them in many ways—all with the best intention ; but unfortunately, with quite an opposite effect from what he intended, for the children came to con-sider him a bore, and liked to play tricks upon him.

This last trick offended him very much, and he resolved to give up trying to please the children for the future.

When Aunt Kate recovered from her fright, she could not help teasing Mr Brown about his "eelegant" gift, and so on, until at last he got quite low-spirited ; and although he had intended remaining with his sister for a few days at Glenmorven, he hastily bade them good-bye, and set off in his steam launch, which was still in the bay.

CHAPTER IV.

NEXT day, having got Mr Farquhar's consent, the twins and Tom went to consult old Sandy, the grieve, about the bonfire.

Sandy was a tried friend of theirs, had helped them in many of their undertakings, and had got them out of many scrapes. He had one rather tiresome peculiarity—he could never give a direct answer to a question ; so that getting information from him was always a work of time. However, they got out of him at last, that an empty tar barrel, a large quantity of dry brushwood, and a plentiful supply of shavings and chips, were the chief materials required for making a successful bonfire.

Sandy entered with his usual good-nature into the scheme, and promised to give them his assistance, by providing the tar barrel. He also told them in what part of the plantation they would find dry wood, and that they could get as many shavings and chips as they required about the sawmill.

Tommy, as I said before, attended the parish school, and was a sort of little prince among the farmers' and cottars' children, who looked upon him as their chief, and were always ready to do his bidding.

As this was the "big play," or summer vacation, he could easily get the help of some of them in collecting materials for the bonfire.

The Dun, where they had fixed to make it, was a small hill, with a flat top, rising straight above the high road. A larger hill rose close behind it.

Tommy sent word that very evening to some of the scholars to come to Glenmorven House next morning; while Bel and Fan went to engage some girls from the cottars' families near the farmyard—girls who used to help them with their house building, gardening, and so on.

Next morning the working party assembled; the boys undertook to collect the brushwood, and the girls set off to gather the chips and shavings.

Both parties worked hard; the boys gathered the sticks into bundles, round which a stout rope was tied, and then dragged them to the Dun. The plantation being on a higher hill, the work of dragging them down was not difficult. The girls conveyed the chips in shawls and aprons; and you may suppose both parties laughed, and shouted, and made fun over their task. Towards evening, Sandy, true to his promise, arrived with the tar barrel, and finding a large quantity of materials already collected, he showed the children how to arrange them.

First he laid down a heap of shavings, then some of the smaller brushwood; over this he placed the tar barrel, and over it more brushwood.

Now that the foundation was properly laid, he told the children they might heap on all the remaining materials as high as they could reach. Before dispersing for the night, the erection was so high as to attract the notice of persons passing along the road; and this gave the children much pleasure, as they could overhear any remarks made upon it.

Next morning they set to work again, and continued till the afternoon, when their uncle came down to see how they were getting on, and told them they had now quite enough of wood. So they dismissed their assistants, engaging them to return next evening, when their Uncle Charles was expected to arrive.

I think the children were very glad of the rest, for they had worked very hard; and I daresay it was their tired and heated appearance that had made their uncle wish them to stop.

They spent the evening in talking over their expected fun, until their spirits were a little damped by the arrival of Mr Brown.

That young gentleman had left Glenmorven in rather an offended state of mind; but being really very good-natured, on getting a letter from his sister begging him to return, he had done so.

Next day seemed very long to the children, but at last six o'clock came, the earliest hour at which the steamer could arrive. There was always great uncertainty about the hour of the steamer's arrival : it might be any time between six in the evening and six in the morning; but as the weather was beautiful, they hoped she would arrive in good time, that is, just as it got dark, and when the bonfire would be seen to advantage.

After a hasty tea, the children had hurried off to the Dun, and there they were now assembled, sitting or lying about on the grass, round a tall erection, which looked like the wicker-work baskets in which the Druids kept their prisoners, as you have read of, Nina, in your English history.

About a dozen of the scholars and several girls had joined them. As the steamer could not be seen very far off from the Dun, one of the boys is sent as scout to a point on the higher hill, where he is to wave a handkerchief on the end of a stick whenever he sees the steamer.

As the children lounge about they keep their eyes on the bay, whose waters sparkle in the evening sun, or look aloft for the expected signal.

Now and then, Tom or Fan fancy they see the steamer's smoke, but it always turns out a mistake, and the bay remains still and smokeless.

Presently they see their uncle and Aunt Margaret driving slowly down the road to the shore.

Time passes, and they get a little tired of simply waiting, and begin to look about for some amusement.

Fan notices a wild bee, and follows it a good way, hoping to discover its underground nest. Tom and two or three followers find a wasp's nest in a furze bush on the side of the Dun, and begin to throw stones at it. Bel tells them in vain to desist, being afraid the wasps may fly out and sting them.

The sun sets, and there is a great rosy blush over the sea, sky, and distant hills, for a quarter of an hour, which even the careless children sit still to admire and wonder at. As it fades away, darkness begins to fall, but Fan's quick eye sees two figures coming along the road, one with a white dress.

" Is that you, Aunt Kate?" cries Fan. " Won't you be late for the steamer?"

" There is no fear of that," replied Aunt Kate. " We have just heard that the steamer has to go up Loch Ben with a shooting-party, so she won't be here for a long time yet."

"What a sell!" cried Tom. " I say, that is a down-right shame!"

" I think you had all better go home to bed," said Miss Brown, who was Aunt Kate's companion.

" To bed!" echoed Fan with disdain ; " to bed, after all our trouble ; no, indeed, we shall stay here all night first."

Miss Brown and Aunt Kate laughed and went on.

It was now quite dark, and the children, sitting silent

or talking in low tones, heard the sound of approaching wheels. It seemed to be the noise of a horse and cart moving slowly.

" Hallo! who is that? " called out Tom through the darkness, and the cart stopped.

" And who wud it be but myself? " came in reply.

" Where are you going, Sandy? " called out Bel.

" And where wud I be going, Miss Bel? "

" Are you going down for the luggage, Sandy? "

" And what for wud ye be asking, Miss Bel? "

" Because if you are going to the shore, would you give us a whistle, a very loud whistle, whenever you see the steamer? But be sure it is the steamer; and be sure it is a loud whistle."

" Oh! yes, I'll whustle, Miss Bell; never you fear," called out Sandy good-naturedly, and the cart rattled down the road.

" Who is that going along the road with a cigar, I wonder? " said Fan presently.

" Why, it is old Brown, of course," said Tom hotly. " For any sake keep quiet, or he will be up here in no time."

" What a bore! " said Fan. " Do you think he heard us speaking to Sandy, Bel? "

" Perhaps he might, if he took the trouble to listen," whispered Bel in reply.

" Hold your tongues, girls," whispered Tom. " Can't you keep quiet till he passes? "

When the cigar light came below the Dun it stopped, and then an amiable voice was heard calling—

" Bel ! "

No reply.

" Fan ! "

A pause—then rather louder—

" Tommy, my boy, Tom ! "

Still a dead silence.

Then the voice muttered, " Sulky little beggars ! " and the spark moved slowly on.

CHAPTER V.

IT was beginning to get a little cold, so the twins thought it would not be a bad plan to light a small fire to warm themselves at. They got some live peats from a cottage near, and soon had a bright fire, where it could not be seen from the bay, in the shelter of a small rock, at the foot of the larger hill. When the excitement of lighting the fire was over, and they began to look about for something else to do, they noticed a quantity of dried ferns on the hillside, which the cottars had cut for bedding for their cows. The twins thought if they had to spend the night in the open air, they would make themselves at least comfortable; so they ordered their attendants to bring armfuls of the dry ferns, and soon had quite luxurious couches near the fire.

Lying on these, and watching the glowing peats, they felt like soldiers bivouacking, and were supremely happy.

" Isn't this delightful, Bel?" asked Fan. " Doesn't it seem just like what we read in the *Romance of War* about the soldiers in Spain, when they sat round the camp fires?"

" Yes, indeed," answered Bel; " but I think they always had supper. I feel very hungry."

"Well! so do I," said Fan; "and I think we had better send for some oatcake. I am sure cook will give us some."

So one of the slaveys was sent with a message to the house, and soon returned with a basket full of oatcakes, bringing also a couple of shawls nurse had sent.

Tom meantime had employed himself, with the help of half-a-dozen of the boys, in setting the wasps' nest on fire—a work, as they imagined, of courage and danger. But they felt rather small when not a single wasp appeared, proving that the nest was an old deserted one.

Tom came up to the bivouac just as the oatcake arrived, so he took command, and served out the rations fairly.

When their supper was eaten, they all felt quite refreshed and fit for anything, and wished very much the steamer would now arrive. Hush! what is that distant sound? Their hearts thrilled within them! Again it comes on the calm night air—clearer, shriller, more convincing than before! It is the whistle!—the assurance that the steamer is at last approaching Glenmorven, with Uncle Charles on board.

Now is the time to show the world, the captain, and the tourists, how right royally their uncle is to be welcomed home!

Up sprang the bivouacking party—twins, scholars, Tom, and all. To Bel was entrusted the important task of setting light to the bonfire. The natural effect of agitation and a slight breeze, however, caused a successive number of matches to go out, until, at last, a ready-witted scholar fetched a burning peat, and thrust it into the heart of the shavings. All stand breathless around, watching the result. First a feeble flicker, then a small flame, a puff of wind, and—darkness. Is it possible? Surely not! No! up leaps a stronger flame; the tar barrel catches fire. Hurrah! it crackles and splutters; long tongues of flame shoot up; the children clap their hands; they shout; their faces glow in the light—when the scout, whom they had forgotten, but who had remained faithful at his post, from which he could see the steamer's lights a great way off, came running, wildly shouting out, "What weel ye be doing? what weel ye be doing? The steampoat is not there at all, at all!"

"What! what do you mean?" cried Bel horrified; "but we heard the whistle!"

"Yes," said Tom, "Sandy promised to whistle from the shore when the steamer was seen coming. Didn't you hear him yourself, Donald?"

"Not a whustle did I hear from Sandy, but from another man; and it wasn't from the shore at all," asserted Donald.

"What other man?" asked Bel faintly.

"The Englishman with the white hat, who is always putting windows to his eyes," answered Donald.

"Oh! it's Mr Brown," groaned Tom. "Oh! how mean! how awfully mean! He must have heard us speaking to Sandy."

"It's just him," said Fan in a voice of despair; "and he has spoilt everything."

"Never mind," said Bel stoutly, "let us try and put out the fire; perhaps it is not yet too late. Donald, run to the cottage for a pail, and bring it full of water. Come, all you boys; let us pull down all the big sticks from the top before they catch fire."

So, with the rashness of youth, the children set to work at once to pull the bonfire to pieces. It was of course very dangerous, and had any grown-up person been there they would not have been allowed to do it. A slight breeze blowing the fire to one side left the other easier to approach. The boys seized the long pieces of brushwood, pulled them off the fire, and ran off with them in all directions. Some of the older boys, who had had some experience in putting out burning heather, seized some large branches that had not been put on the bonfire, and beat out the flames with them. Then Donald arriving with water, the tar barrel was drenched, so that in a few minutes the tall bonfire was lying low, and the children could rest from their frantic exertions. Upon the whole, they enjoyed the wild excitement, and fortunately no one was hurt.

After they had rested a while, and the fragments had

cooled, they collected them all again, and with some reserve stock which had not been used for the first, they built them up as well as they could, so that a new bonfire might rise from the ashes of the old. But, alas! they sadly felt that this one would be shorn of half its glory, thanks to Mr Brown.

During this time, the bivouac fire had been neglected, and when the bonfire was as well made up as they could make it, and they retired to their couches for some needful rest, it was all but out. It required much coaxing and blowing before it could be made to burn up again. They grouped themselves about it rather dismally. Yes; it certainly was cold. Some of the scholars who lived far up the glen went home; and the mother of one of the girls came to take her home, and strongly advised Tom and the twins to go home too. But they were resolved to stay till morning, if need be, were it only to show Mr Brown how little they cared for his mean revenge; and Donald and the rest were determined to stick by them to the last.

Fan was getting tired and sleepy, though quite as determined as the others to remain. "The heath this night shall be my bed," sounds very nice in fancy, but is not quite so comfortable in reality. However, Bel made her lie down on a heap of dry ferns, covered her up snugly with a shawl, and Fan was soon sound asleep.

How long she slept she never knew, but in the midst

of a dream in which she, and Bel, and Tom, were pursuing Mr Brown with burning sticks through long, dark passages, she awoke. All was darkness. She rubbed her eyes, then raised herself on her elbow, and saw that she was lying beside a dying fire, and all alone. She lay down again, and presently heard some strange sounds like smothered shrieks. She sat up, and, looking round, dimly perceived on the hillside a number of figures flitting about like witches. She felt quite frightened, and called out—

" Bel ! Bel !"

To her relief, Bel came running towards her.

"Has the steamer come, Bel?" she asked, ashamed to say she had been frightened.

" Not a bit of her," said Bel. " We got tired of sitting still, and went to play games to keep ourselves warm ; and we tried not to make a noise for fear of wakening you. Had you a good sleep ?"

" Oh yes !" said Fan; "and plenty of dreams. I thought we were pummelling Mr Brown with burning sticks."

" And that is just what he deserves," said Bel. " But don't you think you had better come and run about with us to warm you ?"

" Oh no," answered Fan, " I feel rather lazy, and am quite comfortable and warm."

" Dear me, that tiresome fire is nearly out again," said

F

Bel, as she stirred it up, and then went on her knees and blew it, till her face and hair were full of smoke and ashes. However, at last, it began to burn up bright again.

Meantime Fan lay and looked at the sky; it was all a dull grey, no stars to be seen, and no light, except just over the hill on the opposite side of the river, where a pale light over part of the sky let one see the outline of the hill.

Tom, who had continued his game with the scholars, now came rushing up, breathless.

" Bel! Fan! there are Aunt Kate and Miss Brown, and that wretch, climbing up the Dun from the road. I'm not going to speak to him. I say, Bel, shall we throw some burning peats at him?"

"And then have no fire left!" said Bel, who was always practical.

" But I say, girls! you mus'n't speak to him; he is just coming here to see what mischief he has done to our bonfire—the sneak!"

But Mr Brown did not appear to have any such intention. Before the party got to the top of the Dun, they turned aside and began ascending the higher hill.

On seeing the children, Aunt Kate called Bel to come to her; and after a few minutes Bel came running back to tell Fan that the party were going up the high hill to see the sunrise, and, as Aunt Kate said she did not know the best spot, she wished Bel to guide them.

"So you can keep the peats, Tom, till we come back," said Bel, laughing, as she ran off.

CHAPTER VI.

FAN watched them dreamily as they climbed up the hill; the one small figure and the three bigger ones, Mr Brown's white hat continuing visible after the rest of his figure had gradually faded out of sight.

Meantime the faint glow in the eastern sky was growing brighter, and spreading more and more.

" Oh, bother it ! " exclaimed Tom suddenly, " the sun will be up before the steamer comes, and what kind of a bonfire can we have then ? "

Donald came up to him and said, " I think myself I see a light far away."

They all looked, but could see nothing; so Donald speeds away to his former look-out to make sure. Just then a loud whistle reaches the children's ears. Warned by their former experience, they are afraid to trust it. But a joyful shout is heard; Donald comes tearing down the hill, calling out—

" The steampoat ! the steampoat ! it's herself this time, for sure, and no mistake at all ! "

There is no mistake now; there are the glowing lights already shining in the bay, and the throbbing noise of the steam-engine can be distinctly heard.

In a tremendous hurry the children fall to lighting the bonfire. But "the more haste the less speed" is an old and true proverb ; the peats obstinately refuse to do more than smoke ; the whole supply is pushed into the heart of the bonfire ; the whole remaining matches have died out. Half-a-dozen boys throw themselves flat on the ground, and blow, and blow, till they are black in the face. At last Fan brings a handful of dry shavings she has fortunately discovered ; the boys blow with the energy of despair. A tiny flame appears—grows bigger. A boy brings a bundle of dry ferns ; the remains of the tar barrel begin to kindle. Oh, joy ! there is yet hope ; the flame ascends higher and higher !

Just then, Bel came running down the hill like a whirlwind, calling out—

" Is it really the steamer ? You know we couldn't see the bay from where we were."

"Oh, Bel !" cried Fan ; "we've had such dreadful work to light the bonfire ! "

" Just think what Mr Brown said on the hill just now. He said, 'There are those absurd children lighting the fire again, just for the pleasure of putting it out.' So I ran away, and left them to come down by themselves."

" The pleasure of putting it out !" echoed Fan and Tom, quite aghast at this new proof of Mr Brown's malignity.

" But it's doing beautifully now," said Bel cheerfully ;

" the flames are up near the top. But," continued she, after glancing towards the bay, "I don't see the steamer !"

The children, whose attention had been quite absorbed by the bonfire, now turned hurriedly to the bay. It was too true; the steamer had disappeared. The children were deeply mortified; all chance of astonishing the tourists was gone. It never occurred to them that the tourists were all snugly asleep in their berths at that early hour of the morning.

The cheerful crackling of the bonfire now attracted the children's attention. It was burning up with a merry blaze; looking rather pale, indeed, in the increasing daylight, but still bright and lively. Their spirits revived.

"Well! it doesn't matter so much, after all, about the steamer," said Bel; "you know we made the bonfire for Uncle Charles, and he will see it at anyrate."

" Oh ! let us begin to dance round it," said Fan ; and they all immediately took hands, and danced and sang and shouted, and I think after all really enjoyed their bonfire, in spite of Mr Brown.

As the carriage containing Mr Farquhar, Aunt Margaret, and Uncle Charles, came up the road, and a sudden turning brought them in sight of the Dun, I think Uncle Charles was considerably astonished at what he saw. Aunt Margaret, seeing nothing of the bonfire when the steamer was in the bay, had thought the children must have gone home, and to her the sight was also unexpected.

On the Dun, close above them, crackled a flaming pyramid. Round and round it, nay, as it seemed, through and through it, circled, and skipped, and flitted a dozen or so of strange figures, all of them with flying hair, short skirts (most of the scholars wore their hair long, and they all wore kilts), naked and capering legs; shouting, laughing, yelling, singing. As soon as they noticed the carriage, they all rushed to the edge of the Dun, and shouted out—Hurrah! hurrah! hurrah! as loud as they were able.

"What in the name of wonder does all this mean?" exclaimed Mr Charles Farquhar.

"Oh," said Aunt Margaret; "it is only the poor children, the dear creatures, that are welcoming you home."

"They had set their hearts on making a bonfire," said Mr Farquhar, "and have taken endless trouble about it; but I had no idea they would have remained out till now."

"Do you mean that these are Kenneth's children?" asked Mr Charles Farquhar, quite shocked, as the twins in a state of wild excitement ran down the hill. They certainly were "figures;" their hair all loose, their faces blackened with smoke, their frocks so very short. They evidently had intended to have thrown themselves into Uncle Charles' arms, but a look at his face checked them.

"This is Uncle Charles, dears," said Aunt Margaret. "Come and shake hands with him;" which they did.

He was something like their papa; but had no beard, and quite a different expression.

"It strikes me that young people should be asleep in bed, instead of catching cold on the hillsides at this hour," he said reprovingly.

This speech quenched the high spirits of the twins as effectually as the pailfuls of cold water had quenched the tar barrel. Their eyes filled with tears; they had not a word to say.

Was it for this they had toiled for three days? For this they had endured cold and heat? Not one word of thanks or praise; only cold reproof.

They were on the point of beginning to sob, when their old uncle, seeing their distress, and having noticed the near approach of Aunt Kate and the Browns, proposed that he and Uncle Charles should get out of the carriage and join them in walking home.

As soon as they were gone, Aunt Margaret made the twins get in beside her; then calling Tommy, who, seeing something was wrong, had kept at a respectful distance, to come near, she told him to bring all his assistants up to the house, so that each might get a bowl of hot porridge and milk before going home.

"Now dears," she said to the twins, kissing each

warmly, "we shall drive quickly home, and get cook to prepare the porridge."

Nurse had hot milk waiting for the children, so after taking some of it, they tumbled quickly into bed, though it was now full daylight; and you may be sure their dreams, if they had any, were a curious jumble of bivouacks, steamers, scouts, and bonfires.

THE HAY TEA.

CHAPTER I.

"AUNT MARGARET!" cried Fan, running one afternoon into her aunt's room, "do you know that the lawn behind the house has been mown for a long time?"

"Yes, I ordered it to be done; but what about it?"

"Oh! you know quite well, Aunt Margaret; we want to have our Hay Tea."

"I thought as much," said Aunt Margaret, smiling; "well, I shall think it over."

"Oh! but do let us have it now," said Bel, who had followed Fan into the room; "the hay will be quite burnt up, if it is not raked together soon."

"Or rain may come and spoil it, perhaps," resumed Aunt Margaret, still smiling. "Let me see; to-morrow it can't be, for various reasons; the day after, the Browns are leaving, and the Waltons may perhaps arrive."

" Oh ! but it is not quite certain that the Waltons come on Friday, darling Aunt Margaret," pleaded Fan. "I think you better let us have it now. You know if it is put off, one thing and another may come in the way, and then we shall have to go off to Brighton without having had our Hay Tea at all."

This last was a powerful argument with Aunt Margaret, for she had never become quite reconciled to the twins having been sent off to a strange school in that hasty manner.

" Well, dears, unless the Waltons arrive, I really know of nothing to prevent you having it on Friday afternoon, provided, of course, that the weather is fine, and that you behave well till then."

" Thank you, oh, thank you ! darling Aunt Margaret, we are sure to be good ;" and the twins threw their arms about their aunt's neck, and gave her a dozen kisses.

" How many children may we ask ?" inquired practical Bel. " There are the miller's children, and the school-master's boys, and the smith's girls, and the cottar's children."

" And all the schoolboys that were at the bonfire," broke in Fan.

" Stop, stop !" cried Aunt Margaret, " I cannot have a mob. You must confine your guests to girls, and a few little boys. A tea party on the lawn is different from a game on the hillside ; but be sure to remember this, that unless you are good, you can have no Hay Tea, so I advise you to play no fresh tricks on Mr Brown, for I have noticed some whispering going on, and some sly looks directed to him."

Bel and Fan coloured, but said nothing.

"Well, well," continued their aunt, "I hope you will behave well for the next two days. You can run away now, for I am busy ; but," she added seriously, "I again advise you to let Mr Brown alone."

"Let Mr Brown alone ! indeed, I wish he would let us alone ! " exclaimed Fan, when they had left the room.

" But you know he has been much better lately," said Bel; "in fact he never looks at us now, nor at any one but Aunt Kate."

" Oh ! but that is bad enough," said Bel. "Aunt Kate is not half so nice to us as she used to be. She never has any time to play with us now. She is always going to walk with Mr Brown ; or to play to Mr Brown ; or something. However, Mr Brown goes away to-morrow, and we must tell Tommy to throw away the frog he was keeping to put into Mr Brown's bed to-night."

You say you don't know what a Hay Tea is, Nina ! Well, it is perhaps not a very good word for it ; but it was a little feast that the twins had been allowed to hold all the years they had been at Glenmorven.

At one side of the house there was a largish lawn. Just under the windows there was a flower border, next a broad walk, and then the lawn. A few trees dotted it here and there, and it ended in a belting of fir. The far part of the lawn was rather wild, but the part next the house was mown now and again. It had once or twice happened, that when the farm people were very busy, Aunt Margaret, who did not like to see things look untidy, had set some of the cottar's children to rake up the hay, giving them afterwards tea, as a great treat ; and this was the origin of the Hay Tea.

The twins and their little friends were first expected to rake up the hay very carefully, and when they had gathered it all into a large flat hay cock, a cloth was spread over this, and they were regaled with tea and oatcakes and jam.

Bel and Fan were this time looking forward to their annual festival with as much delight as ever ; but alas, several unfortunate things were to happen before Friday evening.

The twins ran away to find Tom and tell him the good news. They searched and called about the house and garden in vain. Then they went to the stables, and heard there that Tom was helping in the large hay-field, where all the people were very busy. So down to the hay-field the twins went. The hay had been dried and made up into small hay cocks, ready to be carried to the barn. The day was very hot and sultry, but not bright ; a large dark cloud in the southern sky threatened rain, and all the farm people were loading carts with the hay, that it might all be secured before the rain came on. It was a busy scene; the men worked in their shirt sleeves; the women had on dark petticoats, bright cotton jackets, and sun bonnets or handkerchiefs on their heads. In each cart stood a woman, who caught the hay that was being constantly pitched up to her by half-a-dozen men and women; and it was curious to see how the hay in the cart grew into quite a tower, with the woman always on the top of it. And when it was high enough, some of the people spun ropes of hay, with which they bound the loaded cart so firmly that the tower was quite secure from falling while being carted home. Some children followed each party, raking up the scattered hay. It was dreadfully hot, and the people worked their hardest. Yet they were very merry, for hay-making always seems a kind of rough play. These kindly people were all good friends of the twins, and, many a blessing and many a good word they got from them as they ran across the field.

CHAPTER II.

THE twins could see Tom nowhere; but the hay-makers told them he had been there a short time before, so he could not be very far off. They had reached the far end of the field, still shouting " Tom ! Tom !" in vain, and were on the point of returning, when, at last—

" I'm here," was heard from behind a hay cock.

" What are you doing?" called both girls together.

" Munching and mousing" was the singular reply.

" What can he mean?" said Fan.

They found Tom lying full length in the shade of the hay cock, evidently extremely comfortable, and eating an apple.

" Well, Tom ! you do seem to be working hard," cried Bel ironically. " Aunt Margaret likes us to work when they are in a hurry with the hay, because she says, ' Every little helps ;' but I think your help is certainly very little."

" Oh ! but I was helping," Tom replied indignantly. " Just you ask Murdoch ; I worked until I was quite tired, and came here for a minute to rest. What do you think I have found?"

" How can I tell; but do show us, Tom ; you know we always show you our things."

" Well, be careful then ! What do you think of that ? five little mice in a nest."

Wasn't that something to see, Bertie ! There they were, in a round nest of hay, lined with a kind of cottony stuff, five wee, tiny, naked mice, quite pink, with only a few little white hairs, and quite blind. You never saw such odd little creatures.

" Well," said matter-of-fact Bel, after they had sufficiently admired Tom's treasure ; " what are you going to do with them ? "

" I'll put them in a cage and keep them," said Tom.

" But they'll die without their mother, and you can't catch her, you know," said Bel.

" Oh, but I can catch a mouse in the house, and that will do just as well ; you know the old hen-wife takes chickens from one hen and gives them to another."

" Well, I don't know about that, but we can ask Aunt Margaret," replied Bel, looking with compassion at the little creatures.

" I say, girls, wouldn't you like some apples," said Tom ; " I gathered a good many this morning from under the little round tree in the orchard."

" Why, Tom, they cannot be nearly ripe ! "

" But they are though," said Tom. " I don't think they are a very sweet kind, but I like the flavour of them ; the high wind has knocked them off by dozens."

Tom emptied his pockets. The apples were green

and small, and, as Tom said, certainly not a sweet kind. They were, in fact, very unripe, quite bitter, and as hard as stones. The twins, not to be beaten, with much difficulty each got through a small one ; but Tom, though he could not help making faces while eating them, declared they were capital, and very refreshing; he had given some to Murdoch, and he thought so too.

After a while, the people worked up to their corner of the field, and the twins thought they would also give a little help. So they put the mice carefully into a safe corner under a tuft of grass, and all went to help with the hay. The twins worked very well. They were sometimes indeed tempted to throw the armfuls of hay at one another instead of throwing them up to the cart; but, on the whole, they worked steadily. Not so Tommy, who worked very lazily, and at last suddenly sat down on the ground.

" Master Tom's as white as a sheet ! " exclaimed a woman. Fan dropped her armful of hay and turned round. Tom's head had sunk on his breast, and he was the colour of death.

" Tom ! Tom ! don't die, don't die ! " sobbed Fan, running and throwing herself down beside him.

" What's the matter ? " cried Bel, now running up. " Why, I do believe he has fainted," she said, as she sat

down beside Tom, who had now sunk down on the
ground, and raised his head on her lap. "Murdoch,
run and get some water."

Murdoch flew to the river, and was back in a minute
or two, bringing a little water in his cap. As soon as
some water was sprinkled on his face, Tom recovered a
little, opened his eyes, but seemed unable to speak. The
men and women had all clustered about him, consulting
what was best to be done, and at last it was decided
that he should be lifted into the hay cart, now ready
to set off to the barn. Not to disturb the children,
Tom's hay-cock had been the last to be carted off, and
the cart was not half full. So Tom was lifted up on
the hay beside the man in the cart; and Fan, at her
own request, was lifted up beside him. Bel walked
beside the horse.

"Oh Fan! I feel so ill," gasped poor Tom, after
they had gone a little way. "My head is so giddy; it's
all these stewed prunes at dinner!"

Fan strongly suspected it was the unripe apples;
but she did not want to distress him, so she said
nothing, only tried to support him as comfortably as
she could.

Presently the cart, after many a bump and thump,
reached the high road, and went on more smoothly.
Near the house they met Uncle Charles, walking by
himself.

"Who's that on the hay cart?" he called out. "One would think the poor horse had enough to pull without a parcel of lazy children as well!"

One of the lazy children groaned, and tried to raise himself up, but couldn't.

"It's very unkind of you to say that," called out Fan, like a little vixen, from the top of the cart. "I don't think you would say it, if you knew poor Tom was nearly dying."

"Bless my soul!" cried their Uncle Charles, "what has happened? What's the matter with the poor fellow?" he asked Bel, turning and walking beside her. Bel told all she knew.

When they reached the house, Tom was taken down very carefully by his uncle and carried in.

Uncle Charles was not accustomed to children, and thought they must be always scolded; so he often said things that wounded them very much, without in the least intending it, as on the night of the bonfire; but he was really very kind-hearted.

Tom complained so much of his head, and looked so pale, that they were all quite alarmed. Fortunately the doctor happened to be at the village seeing a sick woman, so he was sent for. When he came, he said Tom had a touch of cholerina, from exerting himself too much in the hot sun, and from eating something that had disagreed with him.

After giving some directions, and leaving some nasty-tasting powders to be taken, he went away. As he had ordered Tom to be kept quite quiet, Uncle Charles said he would remain with him and nurse him.

CHAPTER III.

THE twins were very dull all that afternoon, thinking of poor Tom, whom they were not allowed to see. But next morning, on hearing he was much better, their spirits revived. Aunt Margaret even said it was possible he might be allowed to get up a little in the evening. Before hearing this, they had quite believed the Hay Tea must be put off; but now they began to have some hope again. They sat with Tom a good part of the day, read stories to him, and listened to his account of how he felt, and what the doctor said, who would insist that it was the apples; whereas Tom knew it was the stewed prunes that had made him ill. Stewed prunes was a dish Tommy never liked.

In the afternoon Aunt Margaret said Tommy should be allowed to sleep a little, and she told the girls to go out. They went out rather listlessly, for they did not feel inclined to begin any play without Tom; so they betook themselves to the garden.

They first visited the gooseberry bushes. How well they knew the flavour of each kind of gooseberry! The hairy red, with its rich taste; the golden ball, like drops of honey; the large smooth green, so cool and refreshing.

After the gooseberries they went to the strawberry beds, and hunted out a few late strawberries. In general, they were great fruit-eaters, and never were the worse of it; but to-day, somehow, Tommy's illness caused the fruit to lose its attraction; so they soon left it, and went along to the south wall, where their own gardens were. These consisted of two small plots between the walks and the garden wall. They had a number of narrow paths, bordered by white pebbles, which had been the twins' own fancy, and their own work.

The gardens were much better kept than usual, as in the twins' absence the gardeners had charge of them The little gardens were alike, except in not having quite the same flowers. There were, of course, no fine flowers, but some very sweet ones; and there were little circles of annuals which would flower by-and-by.

The pride of Bel's garden was a dwarf Scotch rose-tree. It began quite early in summer to put out its little pale pink buds. In wet and cold weather, these, it is true, did not always unfold, but remained little, hard scentless knots; but in hot dry weather the tree became a perfect bouquet of pretty pink double roses, and with what a perfume! Her mamma's fine Indian attar of roses was not half so delicious, and this little rose-tree bloomed on for months.

Close to the wall grew a row of wallflowers, red and yellow. Fan had the same in hers.

In one corner was a large bunch of mountain pink, which smelt like cloves. In another, a bed of pretty, nodding, dwarf campanilla; a white phlox and some purple larkspur were there too.

In Fan's garden the most admired plant was a hen and chicken's daisy. Well, I am not surprised at your looking astonished, Nina; but I assure you it was there. It was a kind of pink and white double daisy. On each stalk grew a large daisy, and hanging to this, in all directions, grew a number of very small ones. It was certainly a curious flower; and funny too, when there was a breeze, and all these little daisies shook about. Fan had, besides, a yellow auricula, which always looked as if it had been newly powdered over, and which is called from this the "Dusty Miller;" a bed of blue forget-me-nots; a large bunch of white pinks which almost rivalled Bel's roses in sweetness of perfume; a scarlet lychniss. All these flowers had been growing there since the aunts were children, and these little gardens had belonged to them.

After the twins had admired all these treasures, they got tired of being there, and went wandering about looking for something else to do. When they came to the green gate in the wall that led to the orchard, they were surprised to find it locked; but then they suddenly remembered that Mr Farquhar had told them that morning that no one was to go into the orchard without his leave.

"I'm sure uncle need not have locked the door," said Fan; "it would have been quite enough to tell us not to go in."

"I think so too," said Bel; "but, Fan, let us go round to the kitchen garden; it cannot be locked, because there is no lock on the gate."

So the twins retraced their steps. I think I forgot to mention, when telling you of the gardens, that there was a third, a vegetable garden. It lay along one side of the orchard, and, for the convenience of the servants, the gate was at the further side from the orchard, and near the back entrance to the house. The wall between the orchard and kitchen garden was old, and rather out of repair, and there were several convenient gaps in it, through which the children used to pass from one to the other; but on this occasion, not being able to get into the orchard, they were obliged to go round to the gate. The kitchen garden was laid out in the usual manner. Beds of carrots, turnips, and onions; rows of peas and beans; borders of parsley; tufts of sweet herbs.

You wonder what they wanted in the vegetable garden, Nina? Food for their rabbits? I daresay that may have been one reason for their frequent visits; but another was, because they liked to eat the raw vegetables themselves; the crisp carrots, the juicy pungent turnips, the sweetish shoots of the colewort, the tender green peas. Their uncle did not think these, eaten in moderation, were unwholesome; raw beans only were forbidden. After a little deliberation, Bel and Fan decided upon a turnip, and chose a nice small smooth one. After Bel had beaten the earth well off it, she produced a pocket-knife Sandy had made her a present of, and having seated herself upon a wheelbarrow lying near, she proceeded to peel the turnip. Just as it was peeled and cut into convenient slices, Fan, who had meanwhile ran away to gather a few leaves of lemon balm to smell at, returned, and also seating herself upon the wheelbarrow, the two crunched their turnip with great relish.

"Isn't it delicious, Bel?" said Fan; "the last one we had was rather hot, and bit my tongue; but this one is full of cool juice. I wonder how people can spoil vegetables by boiling them, and making them soft and nasty."

"Yes, this is a very nice turnip," said Bel; "but how could one eat cold raw carrots and turnips with hot, soft meat, you foolish girl? You would find it very disagreeable, if you tried it. But, Fan, don't you feel some drops of rain? I am afraid we must go in."

"Oh, bother! it is too stupid to go back to the house. How I wish, Bel, we could go and sit in the umbrella tree! You know uncle locked the orchard gate to keep us from eating unripe apples; but I am sure he would not mind our sheltering ourselves from the rain in the umbrella; that is quite a different thing."

"Well, perhaps it is," said Bel; "but still I don't think it would be right."

Just then the rain came down in a heavy shower, and Fan exclaimed—

"Do come, Bel; if we went to the house now, we would be quite wet before we reached it; and the umbrella tree is so near."

Fan quite forgot that almost as near were the large trees of the back lawn. Bel hesitated, but Fan was already running to the nearest gap in the orchard wall, so Bel followed. They half scrambled, half climbed through, and soon found themselves on the lower walk of the forbidden orchard. Now you know, children, this was very wrong. Their uncle had distinctly told them that no one was to go into the orchard without his leave.

Well, the twins slipped along the walk as quickly as they could in the direction of the umbrella tree, when, just as they got near it, they heard voices, and, what was more, they distinctly distinguished the voice of their uncle. They stood still at once. How they wished the earth would open and swallow them! They crouched behind the trunk of a tree which was close to them. Yes, there was no doubt of it; for they could see parts of three figures, and soon made out Uncle Charles, and then Mr Brown, besides their uncle. They had gone, oh horror! to shelter under the umbrella tree.

I can assure you, Bel and Fan were in a state of mind! They trembled, and dared not even whisper to one another. The shower began to pass. What if Uncle Charles should come out from under the tree! Something must be done. Bel, with a very pale face, made a sign to Fan, and as noiseless as a ghost she glided off towards the gap, Fan following her. They did not dare to go on the walk, but slipped from tree to tree. What a fearful ten minutes that was! Though there were a good many trees already between them and the umbrella tree, every twig that cracked, every leaf that rustled, made them believe they were betrayed.

At last, oh joy! there was the gap. They scrambled through it more dead than alive; hurried across the kitchen garden, ran across the fields, and at last took refuge in the barn, where they hid themselves in the hay. It was a good hour before they got over their fright, and were calm enough to go home to tea.

CHAPTER IV.

NEXT morning was very fine, and when the twins went to their Aunt Margaret's room to wish her good morning, she said, that as the day promised to be so beautiful, and as Tommy seemed almost well again, she knew of nothing to prevent their having the Hay Tea, as had been fixed upon. The twins were delighted to hear this, and ran away immediately to invite their guests. They had actually quite forgotten all about the orchard. But, as you shall hear, they were soon to be unpleasantly reminded of it. Since their return from school, they had been allowed to breakfast with the family; or rather, I should say, they had been obliged to, for they would often have preferred taking a nursery breakfast and running off for all the morning. When they were all at breakfast, Mr Brown said he and his sister would be obliged to leave early in the forenoon, as the steam launch was already in the bay waiting for them. Mr Farquhar pressed them in vain to remain for a few days longer; indeed, he was so hospitable, that, had they been there for months instead of days, he would have pressed them to remain all the same. However, Mr Brown said some business obliged him to go home, and that he was very

sorry to leave Glenmorven, with some polite speeches
about the happiness he had enjoyed there, and ended by
hoping they would all come over soon, and pay him and
his sister a visit. Turning to the twins, he continued,
"and you too, young ladies, if your aunts would be kind
enough to bring you."

The twins said nothing, but looked at one another in
a doubtful manner.

The conversation then turned to shooting, and from
shooting to poaching. Mr Farquhar said they had very
little poaching at Glenmorven, except when some of the
village children stole his apples.

"By the way," said Uncle Charles, "I wonder if it
was a poacher that dropped the knife we found in the
orchard yesterday?"

The twins felt themselves getting quite hot.

"No, I don't think it was a regular poacher," said Mr
Farquhar, looking quite straight at Bel. "The apples
are not ripe enough to tempt a poacher yet; but if any
one stole and ate the unripe apples, I pity him; he
requires no further punishment."

The twins were now sure he knew, and trembled, but
did not speak.

Mr Brown laughed knowingly.

"I'm sure I pity him too, poor wretch!" he said; "that
would be poetical justice upon the spot," and he laughed
again.

"Oh! how hideous Mr Brown looks when he laughs," thought Fan.

"Let us see the knife again, Charles; perhaps it may identify the thief."

Poor twins! it was all over with them; how wretched they felt.

Uncle Charles laid the knife on the table, and Mr Brown having looked at it, handed it to Mr Farquhar.

"It is a very common knife," said the latter; "half the boys in the parish carry such another."

"Is there good fishing in your river this season?" asked Uncle Charles of Mr Brown; and the conversation went on to other things, no one troubling their heads about the twins.

But the poor twins dare not raise their eyes; and as soon as breakfast was over, they ran away to their room.

"Oh Bel! what shall we do now?" said Fan. "Why did we go near the orchard? I was sure uncle had seen us."

"It was very, very naughty of us to disobey uncle, who is always so kind," said Bel. "Oh! how I wish we had not gone."

She felt inclined to reproach Fan for having induced her to go, but, seeing her distress, refrained.

"Oh Bel," said Fan, "how I wish now I hadn't made you go; but what can we do? We must go at once and beg uncle to forgive us; and oh! we cannot have the Hay Tea."

"I don't think we deserve to have the Hay Tea now, Fan. I am sure I don't care about it;" and Bel began to cry.

So the tearful and repentant twins went to their uncle's study: he was not there; but they heard his voice below, saying good-bye to Mr Brown and his sister, whom Aunt Kate and Uncle Charles were going to drive to the shore. It required all their fortitude and re-solution to wait till their uncle came upstairs again, and not run away to hide themselves somewhere, far, far away. However, they waited with beating hearts till they heard him come up, and then they went again to his study.

Their uncle was much surprised at their appearance. "Why, where have you been, children? Mr Brown wished to say good-bye to you, and you were not to be found. But what's the matter? Crying? Why, I hope it's not for Mr Brown!"

"Oh uncle," sobbed Bel, "we were not crying because Mr Brown has gone, but because we are sorry for having been so naughty; and we want you to forgive us."

"And we didn't want to eat any apples; we only wanted to sit in the umbrella tree, because it was rain-ing," added Fan.

"And we know that we deserve to be punished.   We know we do," said Bel; "and I suppose we mustn't have the Hay Tea, for that would be the greatest punishment, because we have looked forward to it so much."

"But what have you been doing, children?" asked their uncle, looking grave.   "Tell me the truth."

"We know we disobeyed you, uncle; and that was Bel's knife.   And indeed we did not want any apples."

Mr Farquhar looked rather astonished, for he had not seen them in the orchard; and it was only their own evil consciences that had made them think he alluded to them at breakfast.

"And the knife was yours! And after I had distinctly told you not to go into the orchard.   This is, indeed, very bad."

"We only wanted to sit in the umbrella tree, dear uncle; and we saw you under it, and then we ran away; and we know we deserve to be punished," and Bel wept afresh.

"But do let them have the Hay Tea, uncle," sobbed Fan.   "Do let Tom and the rest have it; don't punish them for us."

Their uncle was silent for a minute, and then he said, "Listen to me, children. I think disobedience a very great fault, but there is a worse; and that is, telling lies. I don't mean to say that it was not very wrong and very heedless of you to disobey my orders. I hope such a thing may never occur again. But I am glad you have told me the truth about it. Always do that, my children! Whatever faults or mistakes you may commit, always confess them boldly. I would have been better pleased if you had come and confessed yesterday, before you knew the knife had been found. However, better late than never. I shall punish you, of course; for you deserve it. But you shall have the Hay Tea. Not to let you have it, would be punishing others as well as you; and without you the others would not enjoy it. Here are some seeds which have been knocked down, and all mixed together. You must remain here quite quiet for two hours, and arrange them."

" Oh, dear uncle! you are too, too good," cried the twins.

So they sat on the ground, and began arranging the seeds, while their uncle took out his watch to note the time. The first hour passed quickly, but the second was really a punishment; for the twins were obliged to sit still and silent in the dull room, while the sun shone and the birds twittered outside. Only once, when their uncle crossed the room to fetch something, he patted Fan's head and said—

"So you wanted Tom and the rest to have the fun, though you couldn't?"

At last he told them the time was up, and they might go.

H

CHAPTER V.

ABOUT three o'clock that afternoon, many busy figures might be seen on the back lawn raking up the hay, first into small heaps, which were afterwards to form a large mound, near the drawing-room windows. The younger children of the house were there also, rolling and tumbling about on the hay. Chatty was now a big girl of eight, and almost getting past nurse's control. No prisoner ever longed for freedom, no bad sleeper ever longed for morning, more earnestly than Chatty longed for the day that would see her no longer a nursery child.

For in most children's lives there are three stages— the nursery, the schoolroom, and the drawing-room. How the nursery child longs for the schoolroom, and how the school girl longs for the drawing-room! I cannot say the twins did so yet; but it would come, like other things.

Tommy was there too, but not allowed to work; he sat in a chair, wrapped up in a shawl, and kind Aunt Isa sat beside him. You may be sure it was very hard for him to resist jumping up when he saw some of the others burying one another in the hay, or making some such fun; but he had been only allowed to come out on condition that he would sit still.

It was thought a splendid idea when Bel proposed that they should make a circular mound or bank of hay outside the central one, which would serve to sit on while the other was used as a table. They all set to work to make it, Tommy shouting directions from his chair. After a couple of hours of hay-making, when every one was hot and tired, cook and nurse appeared on the scene.

Nurse came first, carrying a tray on which was a very large jug, surrounded by numerous small mugs.

Cook followed with another tray, containing several large plates, heaped up with oatcake and jam. Bel ran to meet them, and taking a white tablecloth which nurse had on her arm, she spread it on the central haycock. The tray of oatcakes and jam was laid on it, but, as it was not considered quite steady, nurse thought it advisable to keep the other tray in her own hands, until the children all came round, and each took a mug. Cook said a few words to Aunt Isa, who rose and went into the house. The large jug contained the tea, ready creamed and sweetened ; and Aunt Margaret herself having made it, you may be sure it was good. The twins felt a little disappointed that Aunt Margaret did not come as usual to pour out the tea, and divide the oatcake and jam. But nurse told them that the Waltons had just arrived, so she had been unable to come. The twins watched nurse very narrowly while she dispensed the good things, for they knew she was always displeased at their being allowed to play with the barefooted country children. Though she had been so long at Glenmorven, being originally from the South, she did not understand Glenmorven ways. It had always been the custom there to let the children of the house play with the children of the cottars and the workpeople. These country children were simple, well-mannered, respectful, and quite well-behaved; besides, there were no other children to play with. But nurse would not see this; and, had she been allowed her own way, would have sent all these merry, harmless, little barefooted creatures at once to the right about, instead of giving them a happy evening.

However, on this occasion, all she had to do was to pour the tea into the mugs; and whether she did it with a good or a bad grace, did not affect it much. Oh, how good it was, after all that hard work! Our party, Tom and all, seated themselves on the hay divan, but it did not turn out so great a success as had been expected, for some one was every moment slipping down, mug, oatcake, and all, to the green sward. They had no sooner sat a few minutes still than a new enemy appeared, in the shape of clouds of midges; so that some found it more comfortable to walk about while they took their tea; others, who did not mind the midges so much, built themselves separate and more solid little haycocks, and sat thereon. Presently cook appeared with a fresh supply of oatcake and jam; and then, while the children were all crowding round to get some, Mr Farquhar, Uncle Charles, the Aunts, and two strangers—a tall young gentleman, and a boy a little bigger than Tom— appeared. They had been watching the children from the window, and then, as grown-up people often do, had come out to see the children "enjoy themselves," forgetting that the children's enjoyment would cease with their presence. The children became at once shy and silent. The twins and Tom were introduced to the Waltons, whom they had never seen before. I am afraid the twins looked rather sulky, for they were put out at being interrupted.

After walking about and making a few remarks, the party went away to the garden, Aunt Margaret telling Tom to go in directly he finished tea, as he might see what was going on from the drawing-room window, and he had been out long enough. Aunt Margaret had brought them a second jug of tea; so when the big people left, they got their mugs replenished, and finished their bread and jam.

Just then old Sandy appeared with the pony cart, to carry off the hay; and as he stooped for the first armful, was it not fun to cover him up with what had lately formed the tea table—Sandy letting himself fall, and pretending to be quite helpless, and half-smothered, while they piled the hay higher and higher on him? The children shrieked with laughter at Sandy's repeated "Let me oot! Let me oot!" At last, when he thought they had had enough of fun out of him, he shook himself free of the hay, and they all helped him to fill the cart.

Soon after, Aunt Margaret came out with a large basket, gave a couple of biscuits to each child, and sent them all home, and so ended the Hay Tea.

THE PETS.

CHAPTER I.

IT would be difficult to tell you, Nina, how many pets the twins had at various times, but I will tell you of as many as I can remember.

" Did you know the twins then, cousin ? "

" Oh yes, Nina; I knew them when I was little. How else could I know so much about them ? "

The first pet that I can recollect was an old jackdaw ; he was also the longest liver. He lived, I think, for three years. I do not remember how the children got him, but he belonged to Fan. He was the most comical looking bird you ever saw. He never walked straight, but always hopped along sideways, as if he was after some mischief ; which indeed he generally was, for he was a great thief. His abode was in a tree near the house. When he wanted to see a little of the world, or to enjoy a little change of air, he removed occasionally to a particular window-sill, but he always slept in the tree. On fine afternoons Fan used to give him a bath. She used to fill a tin basin with water, and lay it on the gravel walk in front of the house, then begin calling kaa-aak, kaa-aak, which is the kind of cry a jackdaw makes. In a minute or two this queer-looking bird came shuffling along—not in a straight line, but in a kind of circle. He had no tail to speak of, and the story was, that he once had had a dreadful fight with a clocking hen, and that she had pulled out all his tail feathers, which never grew again. I do not say this was true, but such was the story ; and certainly Jack had nothing of a tail.

So he would come hopping out of the shade of the tree, looking about him slily, for he did not like strangers ; and when satisfied that only friends were there, he would come quite near, and then flutter up and sit on Fan's shoulder, and seem to whisper into her ear like an evil spirit. But all he really did was to give little pecks at her cheek and hair, which was Jack's way of kissing. There certainly could not be a greater contrast than between poor Jack's ungainly, dusky figure and Fan's bright hair and pretty little fair face; and Aunt Isa could never bear to see her with Jack on her shoulder. Neither could nurse. But then nurse hated all their pets—" nasty aggravating beasties," she called them. After exhibiting his affection for Fan in this way, Jack would flutter down to the ground again, hop into the basin of water, sprinkle himself all over, shake his wings, and, in short, enjoy himself very much.

Tommy was once discovered trying to teach the jackdaw to dance. He had set the poor bird on a rail, and, while whistling " Merrily danced the Quaker's Wife," kept time by tapping Jack with a stick, making him hop at each stroke. But Jack had no desire to imitate the quaker's wife, or even the quaker himself : he pretended to be very dull and stupid, and would not learn.

But Jack was not stupid, for if he found himself near anything bright and glittering, true to the instincts of his race, he would immediately seize it, carry it away, and bury it. The twins knew his hiding-places ; and if a teaspoon or brooch was missing, they went and inspected his holes, and sometimes found the missing things. Jack was once in great disgrace with nurse, and " aggravated " her very much, though quite innocently. Some of the nursery spoons were not to be found, and nurse laid the blame at once on Jack.

The twins thought it likely enough he might have taken them, and searched in all his hiding-places, but in vain ; there was no sign of the missing spoons. They watched him closely for some days in case he might have buried them in some new hole, but all to no purpose ; the spoons did not turn up in any sense of the word. Still nurse blamed Jack, though there was no evidence against him ; and even went to Mr Farquhar, accused

Jack of stealing the spoons, and said his neck ought to be wrung.

The twins, with tears, begged of their uncle to spare his life. So matters continued for some time—Jack under strong suspicion, nurse never passing him without saying something like, " Drat that bird, I'd like fine to see him deid," which the twins thought a most unchristian wish.

Where do you think, after all, the spoons were at last found ? At the back of one of the nursery drawers, where no doubt nurse herself had put them when in a hurry !

You may be sure the twins rejoiced at Jack being proved innocent, and crowed a good deal over nurse, who had the wisdom after this to be less open in expressing her dislike to Jack, though she hated him worse than ever.

Sometimes Jack wandered into the house. One day when they were all at lunch, their only visitor, a stout little clergyman, who had been at Dunard before Mr Murray went there, and who was very prosy, stopped to draw breath in a long speech, when a loud kaa-aak, kaa-aak, suddenly sounded from behind his chair. He jumped up in a fright, not diminished when a dark weird-like bird fluttered up from the floor. The rest, of course, all had a great laugh at Jack's unexpected appearance, in which the clergyman joined after a minute or two.

Poor old Jack ! he died at last.

One day when Fan came to give him his bath, he did not answer her call, and, on a search being made, he was found lying at the foot of his tree, stiff and dead.

Whether it was cold he died of, or old age, no one knew. The twins always believed that he had been killed by a very savage sheep-dog belonging to a shepherd; but if so, he must have died of fright, for he had no wound.

He was buried with great pomp in the pets' burial-ground on the hillside.

You are surprised at the twins burying a bird, Nina! That was another custom of the children of Glenmorven. The twins only did what their uncles and aunts had done before them; for the burial-ground was established long before their time, and displayed many green mounds covering the remains of dogs, cats, rabbits, and the various pets of a former generation.

CHAPTER II.

WHO came after Jack? Well, let me see.

One day a shepherd brought Bel a young sparrow-hawk he had found in a nest, in some steep rocks on the top of a high hill. It had no feathers when it first came, and was like a downy ball, with two fierce bright eyes in the middle of it. It was put into a cage, fed twice-a-day, and grew very fast; but from its earliest youth it showed its savage nature, and constantly tried to bite the person who fed it. As it grew older, beautiful bright feathers replaced the down, and "Sperrack" became a very handsome bird. When it was three months old, Sandy made a new cage for it of solid wood all round, except in front, where there were wooden spars. Aunt Margaret covered the top and sides with moss, and the cage, being fastened below a tree on the back lawn, looked very fine. Visitors were always taken to see the bright plumaged bird sitting gravely in its mossy cage. There was no fun about Sperrack: he was sulky when people went to look at him, and he was savage if he did not get as much food as he liked. Cook always grumbled at the two large pieces of meat a day she had to provide for him; yet he was a splendid bird, and every one admired him. Bel thought him the most splendid bird that ever flew, I was going to say, but Sperrack had not much flying. Bel took him out sometimes for a little fresh air, but only after she had tied a stout string round one of his legs, to prevent his making his escape. She had read a great deal about falconry in a large old book of natural history, and she had found there, that hawks wore bright coloured hoods, and sat on ladies' wrists. So she made Sperrack a hood of scarlet flannel, braided with gold thread, and she borrowed a large gardening glove from Aunt Kate, and after hooding Sperrack, used to set him on her wrist, and walk proudly about.

But Sperrack was not grateful; he would take every opportunity of biting Bel. He objected very much to the hood; and was, in short, anything but an agreeable companion or playfellow.

After a while, Bel got tired of merely walking Sperrack about, and thought it was time to teach him to fly at game.

So after carefully studying the article on falconry again, she took him out one day to the garden, and seeing a mischievous sparrow that she thought might be fair game, she untied the string from Sperrack's leg, pulled off his hood, and threw him up in the air. Away flew Sperrack, taking no notice of the sparrow, higher and higher, over the garden wall, up to the hill, and was seen no

more that day. Next day he came hovering over the
house; when he was observed, some food was placed for
him, a piece of which he carried off. Nothing was seen
of him for some days after that; but about a week after
he made his escape, Tommy was heard shrieking, and
on nurse running out to see what was the matter, there
was a large black and yellow bird perched on Tommy's
bonnet (he wore a blue Glengarry, with a scarlet knob or
button). Nurse flew at the bird with a broomstick, and
frightened him away, Tommy yelling all the time.

Whether this was Sperrack, who took the red knob
for a piece of raw meat, or whether it was a strange bird,
remains unsettled to this day; but, at all events, though
Sperrack's cage remained open for many a day, with
choice tit-bits placed there by Bel inside of it, Sperrack himself never more appeared. He probably returned
to his paternal rock, and may have become father of
young Sperracks as wild and fierce as himself.

Then, I think, came the guinea pigs. No; I think
after Sperrack came several families of rabbits, kept in a
barrel at the kitchen door, but they were not very interesting; so we can come at once to the guinea pigs. Do
you know what they are like, Nina? They are funny little
animals, generally white, with patches of brown or yellow,
something like rabbits; but smaller and livelier, with sharp
snouts for noses. The twins had two sent them by some
English cousins, two little beauties; one white with brown

spots, and the other nearly all white. They were at once named Browny and Whitey.

Such things as guinea pigs had never before been heard of at Glenmorven, in the memory of man. All the scholars, of course, came to see them; and almost all the children in the parish, even from distant places; and many old women came to the house just to look at them. The twins were very proud of being the owners of such rarities, and took great pride in showing the piggies off. They made a comfortable house for them out of the rabbit's old barrel, which they were allowed to place near the garden gate. They fed them regularly, and took them out every day for a walk; in fact, took the greatest care of them. But the fates were against them; and, like most pets, the piggies' career was but a short one. One day Browny escaped out of the barrel and was lost; and when they discovered him, what do you think, Bertie?—he was dead! Yes, Browny was dead, there could be no doubt of it; and many a tear was shed over him. They took him to Mr Farquhar, who found his mouth full of monk's hood, and said there was no doubt but that Browny had poisoned himself by eating it. Thus it was no fault of the twins; still it was very sad that he should die.

Bel and Fan resolved to render him due honour, and give him a grand funeral; so they sent for Kurdag and Effie, the girls who used to play with them, Murdoch and Donald, and several others, to form a suitable train of mourners. And they were all real mourners, for they had all seen and admired the piggy, and lamented its sad fate. They then got out an old perambulator. The twins laid an old cushion on the worn-out seat. On this, piggy was tenderly laid, carefully covered with an old black veil. Then they all moved off slowly, two and two, Murdoch pushing the perambulator, and Donald carrying a spade.

I think, if a stranger had met them on the road, he would have been very much astonished, and would have thought the natives of Glenmorven had strange customs. After going down the road a little way they stopped; then each of the four girls took a corner of the cushion on which poor Browny lay, and they all climbed up the hill to the burial-ground. This was a pretty green spot, not far from the pond, the making of which I told you of before. On one side was the little stream that ran out of the pond; and on the other side a bed of tall rushes. Here and there were small green mounds, over some of which were laid flat stones. Here the procession paused; and the cushion was rather unceremoniously let down on one of these flat stones, while the business of choosing a grave began. On this important subject there was a good deal of difference of opinion between Tom and the twins. However, at last a spot was decided on, and Murdoch began to dig. The ground was very hard and stony; and while the boys dug, the twins went to look for a suitable tombstone in a heap of stately rocks, near the burn. By the time they had found a suitable stone, the hole was considered deep enough. So they laid piggie in, heaped the earth well over him, and then Bel, having got an old stump of a knife from one of the boys, proceeded to scratch "Browny" on the stone. This being an interesting piece of work, all the followers clustered round, and watched the forming of the letters. Bel made them as deep as she could; and the last time I was at Glenmorven, B was still distinctly to be seen.

Just as they had laid the stone upon the grave, Murdoch said that the cows were coming along the road on their way home, and were snuffing and poking at the perambulator. On hearing this, they all set off post haste down the hill, drew the carriage to the house, and felt that everything had gone off well.

Next day,—ah! can I go on?—next day, Whitey was dead. Was it a broken heart for Browny's loss? Was it that she had been neglected during the funeral? Who could tell? The twins couldn't; but there lay her poor pretty little body; and she was dead!

The children comforted themselves as best they could, by giving Whitey just such another funeral as Browny had. Kurdag and Effie and the boys thought it very pleasant; because after the ceremony was over, the

twins had always something nice to divide among them—
a basket of gooseberries, or apples, or biscuits; something
like that. Aunt Margaret wished them not to neglect to
give the poor children, who seldom got a treat, something good on such occasions.

There were no more pets for some time after the
deaths of Browny and Whitey. The twins had been so
fond of their guinea pigs, that they felt their loss more
deeply than that of many other pets. But one day they
went up to the plantation with Sandy. He wanted some
wood to mend gaps in the hedges, and in one of the
small trees he had fixed to cut down there was a nest.
Fan clambered up to look at it, and found it full of
little birds; so they resolved to carry the nest and birds
home. They felt sorry for the disappointment to the
mother, when she should come back with food for the
young ones, and find them all gone; but as the tree was to
be cut down, it was doing a good action to take the nest
home, and preserve the lives of the five little thrushlings
within it. Fan begged that they might be hers; and Bel,
who was always good-natured, agreed to it.

On getting home, she put the nest in a flower pot. No
birds could be more carefully looked after than these were.
When the sun shone, the flower pot was put out on the
window sill; and when it was cold at night, Fan wrapt her
woollen muffler round, and over the birds. She fed them
carefully every two hours with dough, and sometimes

gave them a worm Tommy brought her. She thought it rather vulgar of them to open their mouths so very wide, so she gave them the very smallest morsels at a time, to teach them better manners. At last they came to know her, and whenever she went near them they would begin to chirp, to gape, and flutter. The aunts called Fan the thrush-mother, from her devotion to her birds. They throve very well; that one fell over the nest one day on to the window sill, and from thence to the ground, and was killed, did not matter very much, because it made more room in the nest for the others; and Fan never saw its body—probably the cat carried it off. So, as I say, they were growing fat and strong, until unfortunately Fan and Bel went from home.

They went to pay Miss Murray their promised visit. The thrushes were left under Tommy's care, and every one in the house promised to be kind to them.

The twins enjoyed their visit very much, and returned home very late on the second day.

Early next morning, before they were quite dressed, they heard Tom's voice calling out, " Fan, Fan ; there's something the matter with the birds; come down quick ! I think they are dead."

Fan rushed downstairs, overcome with dismay. It was, alas ! too true; two of the thrushes were quite dead, and the other two were feebly, feebly chirping. Poor Fan took them in her lap before the kitchen fire, and tried to warm and revive them, but it was of no use; very soon the last two stretched out their little legs, became cold and still, and died. Fan sat all morning with them in her lap, weeping. Every one was sorry for her. While she was away, they had been killed by kindness. Tommy had brought them worms almost every hour. Chatty had fed them constantly with bread crumbs. Aunt Margaret had given them their usual allowance of dough; and these stupid little birds were always ready to chirp, and to open their beaks wide for more. So their greediness was the cause of their untimely end.

But I think we have had enough of the pets now. When I resume my stories, I must have a more cheerful subject.

THE COUSINS' VISIT.

CHAPTER I.

DARESAY you would like to know, Nina, who sent the guinea pigs to Bel and Fan? It was their English cousins, Jin and Harry Walton. Jin is a curious name, is it not? Jin's real name was Eugène; but being a French name, and troublesome for English tongues to pronounce, it had been turned into Jin.

The children had never met before, although they had heard a good deal about one another; and it was the Waltons' first visit to Glenmorven.

Jin was a tall lad of sixteen, and he thought himself quite grown up, I can tell you. He had been for a number of years at a great public school in the south of England. Harry was several years younger, and had been for some time at the same school.

The Waltons arrived, as I mentioned before, on the evening of the Hay Tea. After the first words of welcome were over, Aunt Margaret took Jin to the drawing-room window, and said,—

"Look, Eugène, there are your cousins. I don't mean all these children," she added smiling, seeing Jin's alarmed and astonished face. "I mean those five with shoes and stockings on. That's Tom in the chair; he has been ill, poor little fellow!"

"And the twins?"

"The twins are the girls with long fair hair. It is Bel who is carrying an armful of hay, and Fan who is standing under the tree. The little girl in white is Chatty, called after Aunt Charlotte, you know; and the little fellow who has tumbled down is baby."

"And who are the others?" asked Jin.

"Oh! they are the children of the workpeople and cottars on the estate. They are having a little annual tea party on the lawn."

"I was at first afraid you were going to introduce them all as cousins," laughed Jin.

It was now proposed that they should go out and see the children enjoy themselves, as we have seen ; and when they reached the lawn, the children were called to be introduced to, and to shake hands with, their cousins.

Tom looked doubtfully at tall Jin, and the twins pouted and looked shy. They said nothing beyond a formal "How do you do?" and felt very much relieved when the whole party moved off to the garden.

That night, when going to bed, the twins made the following remarks to one another :—

"Well, Bel, what do you think of them?"

"I hardly know yet. I think Jin looks very proud. I had no idea he was so tall. I think he is very handsome. Did you ever see such beautiful fair hair? And oh! what a lovely black velvet jacket!"

"Oh! but Harry's jacket is just as pretty; and I think he looks much nicer than Jin. I am sure I shall like him best."

Next morning at breakfast the twins watched their new cousins very critically. Harry sat quite demure and quiet, never speaking but in answer to a question. Jin talked a great deal to the grown-up people. He had much to tell them about his family and school, and no subject could be started but he knew all about it.

The twins listened breathless with surprise when he argued with Uncle Charles, and appeared to know better than Mr Farquhar. He seemed to have a great deal of humour too, and said things that made them all laugh, though the twins did not see the fun; but that was not surprising, as they were not grown up, and Jin used so many words they had never heard before.

After breakfast, they were running off to play as usual, when Aunt Margaret stopped them, and said it was their duty to amuse their cousins; and they must ask Jin and Harry if they would not like to see over the place.

So the twins, rather against their wills, first asked Harry, who was standing near, not knowing what to make of himself, and he gladly agreed to go anywhere with them. They then went to the inner hall, where Jin was critically examining a long fishing-rod. When Bel timidly made her proposal, he looked down at her grandly with his supercilious blue eyes.

"Thanks very much, but I can't go pottering about with you girls just now. I'm going to fish with Uncle Charles," he said loftily.

The twins, you may be sure, did not repeat the invitation; they were quite sensitive enough to observe his contemptuous manner, and had quite spirit enough to resent it; and so they called Tom, and went off with him and Harry to their own play.

Harry seemed a very nice boy; he had wonderful manners, so polished and polite. At first he always gave odds to the twins in their games, because they were girls— a proceeding they did not at first at all understand, and when they did they were very much annoyed at. They maintained it was not fair, and they would either play fair or not at all.

They initiated Harry into all their sanctums; took him up to the barn, and showed him their favourite play of climbing up a long ladder, and jumping from its top across to a heap of hay. This was a slightly dangerous amusement, because if you jumped short, and did not reach the hay, there was the certainty of falling on the hard stone floor of the barn, and perhaps breaking an arm or leg, if not your head; but the danger added zest to the amusement.

They took him to the pond upon the hillside, and showed him with pride a few small trout that they had managed to persuade to keep alive there; and when there, finding the dam a little damaged, repairing it gave them some hours' occupation. They had then a long consultation about cutting a new channel for the little stream that flowed out of the pond. They had long had the desire to lead it near the garden, and by making it flow through a tile drain, to form a spout or jet, at which they could quickly and easily fill their watering-can.

Then they told Harry the tragic fate of the poor guinea pigs, and showed him where they lay buried.

Next day Harry went with them to the island on the river, and tried his hand at the eel-traps; in short, the twins and he were excellent friends, and were very happy together.

CHAPTER II.

But I am sorry to say that this happy state of things did not long continue. Jin was the cause of it, of course; who but he! Harry had the most unbounded admiration for his big brother, and everything that Jin did he tried in a smaller way to imitate. Uninfluenced by Jin, Harry was a nice enough boy, but when he imitated Jin, and tried to put on airs like him, he was quite unbearable.

Since their arrival Jin had been going about all the time with the grown-up people—walking about with Mr Farquhar, or fishing with Uncle Charles, or chatting with the aunts; for he was fond of ladies' society, though he looked down upon the twins.

Bel and Fan did not mind his taking no notice of them in the least; but when he made Harry and Tommy desert them, and infected them with the notion that it was un-manly to play with girls, they felt it very keenly.

Tom's desertion pained them most. All his life he had been in the habit of looking up to them, and admiring them as much as Harry admired Jin. Now he was always talking in a superior way that hurt their feelings, telling them they knew nothing about this or that, because they were girls!—quite a new sensation to the twins, for they had never before been made to feel that it was a disadvantage to be a girl!

One day Jin offended them very deeply.

Bel and Fan had been sitting on a wall that ran along the road, waiting for Kurdag and Annac, cottars' daughters, who had promised to join them, after having driven home the cows. Getting a little tired of waiting, the girls thought they would climb into a large chestnut-tree that overhung the road, as from its height they could overlook the farmyard. They clambered up a strong branch that hung down close to the wall, and then into a fork nearly half-way up the tree, where they sat down. No cows and no girls were yet in sight; but while sitting there, nearly hidden by the great fan-like leaves, Bel and Fan noticed Uncle Charles and Jin coming along the road. They were returning from fishing, had long rods in their hands, and fishing-baskets slung on their backs. They both looked tired, and Jin was speaking rather crossly to Harry and Tom, who were also there, having gone out to meet them.

" There are Bel and Fan in a tree," sung out Tom, as they came near.

While Jin stared up into the tree trying to see them, his rod and line caught in one of the branches. He shook and pulled, but could not get it free, so he loosened his line, and tried to pull it through. He was cross and angry with himself, his line, the twins, with everything. Fan meanwhile had clambered down to the place where his line had stuck, and was doing her best to set it free, when Jin called out—

"Get away, you little wild cat!" and giving a last impatient tug, the line broke, but not before the hook had torn one of Fan's fingers.

"See what mischief you've done now!" continued Jin rudely; "girls have no business to climb trees like baboons," and he went off after Uncle Charles, who had walked on.

"How rude and cruel!" sobbed Fan; "see how the hook has cut my hand. I had nearly saved his line when he pulled it so roughly."

"I hope he will go away soon," said Bel; "this place has been quite changed since he came; and Tommy has become so stuck up and disagreeable. Harry was nice at first, but now he is nearly as bad as Jin. Oh! I wish they would both go away."

"So do I," responded Fan, as she wrapped her handkerchief round her wounded finger; and thus they bewailed themselves, quite forgetting Kurdag and Annac, until they saw them running down the road. They then descended from the tree, carrying the hook with them; for a real hook, with a fly attached to it, was far too valuable a thing to throw away.

Some days after this, Harry and Tom, not having anything particular to do, and seeing the twins bound for some expedition, asked leave to go with them.

Bel and Fan readily agreed upon certain conditions, which were, that the boys were not to say anything rude about girls; in fact, that they were to refrain from mentioning the word girl at all (the twins had begun to feel it a term of reproach); that Harry was to give up bragging while he was with them; and that Tom was to do as he was bid. The boys agreed to this; and then Bel told them that they were going to visit a cave near the top of the hill, which they had been once at the year before.

"And if you are not nice to us," continued Bel, "we shall leave you in the cave, and you will be obliged to spend the night there or on the hillside, for you won't be able to find your way home."

"We must give them a fright to make them behave themselves," she whispered to Fan.

The boys were duly impressed by Bel's remark; and Harry, resuming his polite manners, offered to assist Fan to climb a steep place they were ascending.

"Oh! never mind," said Fan, "we wish you to think we are other boys—Tom's brothers, for example; and then we shall get on much better."

They had gone a good way, and were scrambling quite amicably and happily together, when suddenly they heard a loud shout from below. On turning round and looking down, they saw Jin.

" Hallo ! where are you going to, boys ? " he called out.

" We're going with the twins," answered Harry.

" And where are the twins going to, pray ? "

" I don't know, exactly," called out Harry; "we're going to see a cave."

" Stop a bit, I'll come too," shouted out Jin ; and to the twins' horror, he began climbing up the hill with rapid strides. It was the first time he had ever joined them in going anywhere, and they did not at all like it. However, there was nothing for it but to sit down and wait for him.

" Where are you all bound for ? " asked Jin, as he paused for breath on getting near them. " I didn't quite catch what Harry said."

" We're going to a cave," said Tommy; " but if you want us to go anywhere else with you, we'll go. We only came with the twins, because we had nothing particular to do."

" Oh ! I may as well go with you, and see this wonderful cave," said Jin, in quite a friendly tone. In fact, as it happened that all the grown-up people were engaged in various ways that morning, Jin had been quite at a loss how to amuse himself, and so was glad to join the twins.

" It is rather a hot day for climbing hills, but I suppose the cave is not very far off."

So they set out again. Although Jin often said that girls were not good for much, he must have felt that day that they were good for climbing; for after some time, when he was quite panting and breathless, the twins were quite fresh and cool.

" Let's stop a bit here," he said presently ; " it's awfully hot. How big is this cave of yours ? " he said to Bel, while he threw himself on the grass.

" Oh ! it's as long as the drawing-room," said Bel ; " but not so broad, nor so high."

" Well, wonderful as it may be, I'm sure it cannot be such a jolly cave as I was once in—it was a stunner ! "

The children crowded round Jin to hear his account of the cave, all except Fan, who could not forget the " wild cat," and who felt a little hurt at Bel for casting such evident looks of admiration at Jin, as he lay on the grass with the breeze playing through his fair hair. He had taken off his cap for coolness.

" Just fancy, Tom," said Jin, " sailing into a cave in a boat. First you go through a dark narrow passage, then you come into the most splendid place you can imagine. The guides have lighted torches and candles of course, and the cave is all lined with sparkling white stone, which glistens and glitters in the light—the very water sparkles. By Jove ! its sumptuous."

The children listen with shining eyes—even Fan becomes interested, and draws a little nearer.

" You've seen a lot of places, cousin Jin," said Tom.

" I've seen a few, certainly; a good many more than you have, you little nigger. I suppose you have never seen any other place than Glenmorven ? "

" But I have though," said Tom triumphantly. " I was born in India; and I have seen thousands of places."

" Oh ! I daresay, when you were a baby; but that doesn't count for much," retorted Jin.

" Were you ever in India ? " asked Bel.

" No, I must confess you all have the pull of me there; but I'm going to India when I'm old enough. I am going into the army."

" Are you going to fight ? " asked Bel, with increasing admiration.

" Yes, my child, to fight; to shoot or to be shot. But, I say, here we are, wasting all the blessed day, and that wonderful cave is not reached yet. You must all of you really look more alive, instead of lounging like this."

Fan could not help thinking this was rather cool of Jin, considering he was the one to rest first.

CHAPTER III.

As they continued their progress, there were many objects of interest that amused them by the way—strange insects and grubs, rare flowers, and here and there a few blaeberries or cranberries.

After nearly an hour's climbing, the twins seemed a little at fault.

" I should be grateful for some shade at this present moment," said Jin. " I'm coming to the conclusion that there's no cave at all; that it is all a delusion and a snare."

" Oh ! you mean you think we told you a lie ? " cried Fan hotly.

" Oh, dear no, young ladies never tell lies. They tell fibs sometimes though."

" We're not young ladies yet; and we don't tell lies, nor fibs either," said Fan. " There ! you see, Bel has found the cave."

There was a bit of hard work yet before they reached the mouth of the cave, which was almost quite hidden by large stones. It was the cave that Bel and Fan had once looked at as a hiding-place, but had found

K

unsuitable. The entrance was very narrow and low, and they had to creep through it one by one; then they came to a large but gloomy cavern. The entrance passage gave a little light, and opposite was a high narrow opening. They had to walk carefully to avoid the stream which flowed through the centre of the cave.

"And you call this a cave in your country?" said Eugène grandly. "Why, it is only a tunnel!"

The twins felt quite humiliated, but had nothing to say in reply.

"Uncle Farquhar thinks it a very curious place," said Bel, at last, timidly.

"Of course, of course; they are all curious places in their way," said Jin.

"And Murdoch says giants used to live here," put in Tom, who had not been before to the cave, and was much impressed by it.

"I wonder how they got in by that passage then?" said Jin.

"Perhaps they got in and out by this end," suggested Harry; but when they went to look out at the narrow opening, they were rather startled to find a sheer precipice below them.

"The giants must have had wings, if they used this entrance," said Jin. "Perhaps they were owls. But what does one do in this hole, when one has got here?"

" We can watch the people passing on the road," said Bel. " You see how small they look; and then we can roll down stones."

Harry and Tom instantly set to work to look for stones to begin an experiment with at once.

" By Jove, it has begun to rain!" said Jin in an injured tone.

" It's a good thing that we got here before it began," said Bel.

" I don't know that," said Jin sharply. " We've got to go back all the way we've come, and it is now," pulling out a handsome gold watch that Bel and Fan gazed at in speechless admiration, " it is now about half-past five. Dinner is at half-past six to-day, is it not? I wonder how people can dine so early! How on earth am I to be back in time to dress, if this rain keeps on !"

There was no help for it, however; the rain kept pouring steadily down, and they must make the best of it. The cave was certainly not a pleasant place to be imprisoned in. A small stream ran through it, water kept constantly trickling from its roof and sides. Everything was damp, and there was no comfortable place to sit on. Fan went to assist Tom and Harry with their stone throwing. Good-natured Bel tried to entertain Jin.

" Fan and I think this would be a splendid place to hide in, if the French were to come over. We could watch them from the opening, shoot at them if we liked, and they would never find us out. It's the most difficult place to find that I know."

" Oh, you needn't be afraid of the French here. You needn't be the least afraid, Bel; the French could never get within hundreds of miles of Glenmorven. We've hundreds of ships always cruising about; and the Mossoos would require to be up very early indeed to get past them."

" But Danes and Vikings used to land here once; uncle has often told us about them; and then the people used to hide themselves in caves."

" Oh, I daresay; but that was long ago. By George!" cried Jin, pulling out his watch again, " it's close on six o'clock; not more than half an hour to get down, and dress and all, and it's raining as hard as ever. Won't that old party in the big cap be wild at your being late again, tearing her hair, wringing her hands, and all that sort of thing?"

" Of course she'll scold us," said Bel; " she always does, but nurse knows we never come to harm. But I think we better really set off home. Fan, Tom, Harry, come along; we're going home now."

It was very wet indeed when they got out of the cave. The large stones and rocks were slippery, and difficult to descend with safety; the damp heather and ferns wet all their shoes and stockings, and their feet slid on the

drenched grass of the hill side. Jin had on that velvet
coat which Bel had admired so much, and it aggravated
him a good deal to think it would be quite spoilt.
Doubtless it was a good lesson to him, for no one but a
conceited boy would have gone about at Glenmorven in a
velvet jacket, or indeed in anything easily spoilt by rain.
Aunt Margaret had given him a hint of this on his
arrival, but he thought he knew best. Consequently
Eugène waxed crosser and crosser, as he floundered
through the wet heather, and felt the rain begin to trickle
down the back of his neck.

He consoled himself by abusing the cave.

"Stupid place! Filthy hole! One could see a much
better tunnel by going on a railway," etc., etc.

Fan, who happened to be near him, as they both
slipped down a wet sloppy bank, could bear it no longer,
and at last said, "I thought you could walk ten times as
far as any girl that was ever born; and here you are, so
much older and bigger than any of us, and complaining
and grumbling the whole time."

"That's a nice way of talking to your elders and
betters," said Jin, with a half laugh. "I am afraid some
important elements in your education have been neglected,
Miss Fanny. Were you never made to learn that admirable precept, that ' little girls should be seen and not
heard?'"

It was this superior way of talking that irritated Fan.

She was not good at repartee. She was too passionate for that. I am sorry to say she had a very quick temper, and often said things she was afterwards sorry for. At this last speech of Jin's, she got red with rage, but tried to restrain herself. Jin gave another half laugh.

"I wonder you don't say 'wild cat,' as you called me in the tree," cried Fan.

"Wild cat! does that afflict you still? You must confess you do behave like a wild cat. Is it like a girl to scramble up into trees like a monkey? I was just saying to Aunt Margaret—"

"I hope you are not going to set Aunt Margaret against us," cried Fan, "and make her keep us about the house. Is it not enough to have to spend nearly all the year far away in a school, without our being tormented in our holidays?"

"But I'm not tormenting you," said Jin.

"But you are tormenting us," cried Fan, giving way to her passion. "You have turned Tom against us, so that he never cares to play with us now. You look down upon us, and pretend you are quite grown up, though you are not much older than we are; and I heard Aunt Kate say you were a conceited boy; and—"

"Stop, stop, Fan, you're a regular little spitfire!"

"I'm not a spitfire, nor a wild cat, nor a baboon!" broke out Fan, getting more and more excited, and bursting into tears; "and I'm not afraid of you, and I'll say what I think and what's true; and I wish you had never come here."

Blinded with rage and tears, Fan stumbled on, and, slipping on a stone, fell to the ground. Jin sprang forward to pick her up. Fan had let her temper get the better of her reason; she was perfectly wild with rage; and what do you think she did when Jin stooped to pick her up?—she pulled his hair! Yes; I'm sure you can hardly believe it, but she flew at him and pulled his fair hair very sharply. When Jin felt the pain he grasped her arm, and gave her a rough shake, which she quite deserved. Fan shrieked, and Bel came running up.

"You wretch, you wretch! I'll never speak to you again as long as I live," were the words Bel heard Fan say as she reached her, while Jin stood looking rather excited, but laughing.

"Nor I either," cried Bel, who always took up Fan's quarrels.

Muttering, "There's always mischief in the wind where there are girls," Jin made off to the house, after Tom and Harry, who were some way on, and had not seen the "scene."

Bel comforted Fan, and soothed her until she gave up sobbing. They made a compact that nothing should induce them to speak to Eugène again. Finally, Fan dried her tears and her face, as well as a damp handkerchief would do it, and they proceeded to the house, where they arrived quite " drookit," as nurse expressed it, when giving them the expected scold. I don't know that they would even have got tea, but that Aunt Margaret, who had heard the outlines of their adventures from Jin, had come to see that their clothes were quickly changed, and that they had plenty of hot tea to keep them from getting cold after such rain.

CHAPTER IV.

AFTER this, the twins avoided Jin's presence carefully. If they saw him in the distance they ran away, and if he spoke to them they pretended not to hear.

Uncle Charles and Aunt Kate had gone to visit the Browns, and Mr Farquhar was nearly all day busy in his study, so Jin found the time hang very heavy on his hands, and was more inclined to be friendly with the twins than he had been when he first came. But it was no use ; he could not even induce them to speak to him. Harry and Tom were there at his service as usual, but he had got tired of them.

This state of things went on for a few days, when, one forenoon, Aunt Margaret begged him to call the twins into the house, as she had something particular for them to do. She had observed a little coolness between the children, but thought it best to take no notice.

Jin had noticed them go into the orchard, which was now re-opened, and he found them sitting in the umbrella tree. Indeed, he heard their voices as he went into the orchard, otherwise he would not have so easily found them out. As he got near the tree, he heard Bel say—

"I say, Fan, there's Jin coming; mind we won't speak to him, or take any notice of him."

"No, indeed; perhaps he wants to come up here to us, but we will show him that we can beat him at climbing, even though he is a man," and Fan laughed mockingly.

"Bel, Fan, come down to the house; Aunt Margaret wants you."

No answer was made by the girls, no movement was heard, and no attempt made to come down.

"Do you hear, girls! Aunt Margaret wants you directly; come down at once."

If Jin had been wise he would have gone away whenever he had delivered his message, but he did not go.

"Do you think Aunt Margaret really wants us?" asked Bel of Fan.

"I'm sure I don't know; but if Jin wants us," raising her voice to make sure that he heard, "he can come and fetch us. We are only girls, you know."

"Fetch you down? I'll do that quick enough," called out Jin, and immediately began scrambling up into the tree.

The girls had really not wanted Jin to come up, although they had uttered that taunt; and they felt very much alarmed at the noise of breaking twigs and at seeing Jin's head appearing in the tree near them. Up stormed Jin like a tornado, and seized hold of Bel before she could make up her mind whether to climb higher, or to creep further out along the branch she was on.

"Now, you're fairly caught, Bel; you're a prisoner of war. Go down to the foot of the tree, and wait there while I go after Fan." Fan was already creeping out along the branch that had formed her seat, and Jin pursued her.

After he had gone a little way, Jin cried, "Now, Fan, give in; the branch will break if you go further. Say you're fairly caught."

But Fan was resolved never to give in. Without answering a word, she kept creeping further and further out, until the branch swung fearfully.

"I'm a monkey, you know, Bel," she called down to Bel, and laughed mockingly.

Jin's blood was up too.

"Come, come, Fan, give in; or, by George, I'll follow you," cried Jin.

No reply from Fan, but another laugh; and Jin began to follow; but before he had gone far there was a groan, a crack, and the branch broke, Fan and Jin falling, of course, to the ground. They had not fallen many feet, and Jin jumped up at once unhurt; but what was his horror to see Fan lie quite still on the ground. Her head had struck against a stone, and she was stunned. It did not help to compose Jin to hear Bel begin to sob and call out—

" You've killed her ! you've killed her ! " as he tried to raise Fan up.

Now Jin's conscience had been troubling him ever since he had given Fan the rough shake. In his lordly way, he thought it unmanly to raise his hand in any way against a girl ; and, in fact, he had done it before he had had time to think. So what was his remorse to find Fan was lying white and motionless, and this his fault.

" What shall I do for her ? " he asked Bel piteously.

" I think she must have fainted," said Bel, recovering her presence of mind. " If we could get water, she might come round. If we were only near our new spout. Do you think you could carry her there ? "

" There's no difficulty in that," said Jin.

So he lifted her in his arms, and carried her out by a back door, and laid her down on the grass near the spout. Just then Fan opened her eyes.

" Fan, darling, are you much hurt ? " asked Bel tenderly. Fan put her hand to her forehead.

" Yes, my head is a little bad. What did you bring me here for ? "

" You fell out of the tree, and we thought you had fainted," said Bel.

Jin saw that Fan was in pain, though she made no complaint, so he steeped his handkerchief in water.

" Let me tie this round your head, Fan ; it will do you good directly," he said kindly, as he tied it on.

" Is your head very bad, dear ? " asked Bel.

" Oh ! it's nothing ; it will soon be better ; " but she closed her eyes as if in pain.

Remorse was busy with Jin.

" Oh ! Fan," he said, " I'll never forgive myself ; let me carry you into the house."

But no, Fan would not let herself be carried ; she would walk herself ; but they had to support her, her head felt so giddy. Fortunately, they met no one before getting to their own little room, where Fan lay down on her bed, and remained quiet for some hours, Bel beside her.

Jin came once to the door, and begged he might be allowed to go and tell Mr Farquhar or Aunt Margaret that Fan was hurt ; but they asked him not to do it, particularly Fan, who said she was almost well. Aunt Margaret had not been much surprised at their non-appearance. She supposed they were not to be found at hand, and afterwards some visitors had come and taken up all her attention. So when Fan appeared in the evening for a short time, and behaved as if nothing was the matter, they thought they could keep the affair a secret. But " murder will out." Next morning there was a large black mark on Fan's brow. Of course every one remarked it ; but to all she gave the same answer, that she had had a tumble the day before. Jin thought it very plucky in her to try so hard to screen him ; but the sight of the ugly bruise at lunch was too much for him: so when some remarks were made about the mark on Fan's forehead, he told the whole story before everybody, taking all the blame upon himself. This was really noble in him, for no one but the twins knew he had had anything whatever to do with it. But, you see, one noble deed induces others to imitate it, and Fan's anxiety to screen him had made him wish to be generous too. No one said anything when Jin was done, except Aunt Margaret, who said, " I should always be told when any accident happens, for this might have been something very serious, and to conceal it was foolish. But I daresay you did it for the best."

The result of Fan's accident was, that, for the first time during Jin's visit, he and the twins were on friendly terms. He continued particularly kind to Fan as long as the least trace of the bruise remained.

He rose in every one's esteem too, by his manly confession of how the accident had happened.

CHAPTER V.

SOME days after this, Jin went to fish in the river, taking the boys with him. Either the sun was too bright, or the fish were not hungry, for after flogging the water for some time, and catching nothing, Jin got tired of it, and came and threw himself down on the grass beside Bel and Fan, whom he found amusing themselves by the river side.

"I wish you would teach me to cast a line, and to tie salmon flies," said Bel. "Sandy has taught us to make fish traps, but he cannot make flies, or fish with a rod."

"That's a modest request," said Jin laughing; "you don't know what you are asking, Bel. You could not hold a salmon; it would either break your rod, or it would carry you into the water. Besides, fly-fishing is not a thing for a girl."

At this hated word Fan looked up.

"And what is a thing for a girl to do?" she asked in a hurt tone.

"Well, I mean what girls generally do," said Jin. "Now, there are my sisters at home; they would as soon

think of asking to be taught to fly as to be taught to fish;
indeed, I think they would prefer the flying, and think it
a more ladylike amusement. I believe they would think
it very cruel to kill fish."

"Do they never eat fish?" asked Fan.

"Of course they do; why do you ask?"

"Because that is just as bad as killing them."

"Well reasoned, Fan; and I am quite of your
opinion."

"Do tell us more about your sisters," said Bel. "Do
they go to school?"

"No; they have a governess at home, and she teaches
them everything under the sun, I think. They play on
the piano in the mornings, and sing like cats gone
mad.'

"Oh, I know," said Fan; "that is practising singing
scales. We do that at Madame Savan's too; and besides,
we learn geography, history, astronomy, botany, the
globes, French, physical geography, drawing, and gymnastics." Here Fan stopped to draw breath.

"My eye and Betty Martin!" exclaimed Jin, "you
haven't much to show for it all then; for I have not heard
you play a note since I came here. Gymnastics. I know,
you may be first-rate at."

"Oh, we left our music at school," resumed Fan; "but
do your sisters learn more than that?"

"Well, I don't know that they learn so much, but

they are somehow quite different from you; they never have torn frocks or rough hair, as you have, for one thing."

"Oh! you should see us at Madame Savan's," said Bel; "there we are always quite neat and tidy. We are obliged to be. Besides, we really work very hard at school; and I think we should be allowed to play all the holidays. It is only two months out of a whole year, and it comes so soon to an end"—and Bel sighed.

" And then we learn so many useful things during the holidays," said Fan. "We can catch fish, and boil potatoes, and do many things that would be of great use in a desert island."

" Desert islands seldom come within the experiences of young ladies," said Jin laughing. "But, halloo! what are those fellows shouting for? Harry, Tom, what is it?"

"A fish—an immense fish!" cried out the boys.

On Jin and the girls hastening to them, they saw a fish lying in a small deep pool, close under the bank.

Outside the pool the river was shallow—the boys were already in the water. Jin ordered the boys to keep quiet, and then he waded into the river.

" If we only had a landing-net," said he, " we could easily catch him; but what's the good of wishing for one?"

"There's one hanging up in the hall," said Fan; "and if

L

you will keep the salmon safe till I come back, I'll run and fetch it."

Fan flew off. The house was not very far from the river, and being a swift runner, in a very few minutes she was back, breathless and speechless, but holding the landing-net aloft. Jin came forward to meet her, took the net from her, and then posting the boys and Bel (who by this time had taken off her shoes and stockings, and was ready to wade in) outside the fish, to prevent its escape, he stepped into the pool. While doing so, he ordered Fan not to come into the water, but to take his rod, and with the thick end of it to poke the fish from under the bank. But to catch the salmon was not so easy as they thought. He made several runs in the direction of Bel and the boys ; he artfully evaded the landing-net many times, just when Jin thought he had secured him ; he hid in the muddy water, that all the commotion had caused; but at last, though not before a good quarter of an hour's hard work, their united efforts were successful, and Jin landed him safely on the shore.

He was not very large, but still he was undoubtedly a salmon, and to have captured him was really a feat.

" If your sisters had been here instead of us, who would have helped you to catch the salmon?" asked Bel, a little later, as the boys, having stuck a stick through the gills of the fish, were carrying him in triumph home.

" Well, I must confess you are better than they are at this sort of thing," replied Jin ; " and the first time I find myself on a desert island, you may be sure I shall send for you."

So the girls and boys were now quite, happy together ; and when, some days later, Jin and Harry were obliged to leave, the girls were very sorry, and felt quite lonely; and somehow their own departure for school, which was now near, did not appear to them so dreadful as it had done the year before, and'they prepared for it with resignation.

" Is it all done ? " asked Nina, after the moment's silence which succeeded my tale.

" Yes ; all."

" Not a ikle bitty mo ?" inquired Bertie, who had taken great interest in the stories, though on some evenings sleep had overcome him.

"No, not a bitty," I replied sternly.

"And it's quite, quite true ?" again asked Nina. "Where are the twins now ?"

" Oh ! they are grown up and married; and Tommy is a big tall man like your papa, and has three little children."

" We've found you out, auntie," cried Nina, after a moment's consideration; "you're telling us of your own selves. Papa's name is Tom, and I've seen Aunt Bella twice, and we have another aunt too ; and— "

"And you're Chatty; for that's for Charlotte, I know," cried sharp little Janet. "We've found you out, auntie! we've found you out!"

"We've found you out!" they all cried in chorus; and so they had.

COMMERCIAL PRINTING COMPANY, EDINBURGH.

www.ingramcontent.com/pod-product-compliance
Lightning Source LLC
Chambersburg PA
CBHW020231030726
47497CB00009B/3040